VAULT OF THE AGES

Carl felt the awe and sadness that lay over the ancient City. It sprawled farther away on every side than he could see. The forest had crept in, and wind and rain had brought the buildings down; wild beasts laired in the wreck and prowled the hollow streets.

But far, far down, the towers gleamed in the sun. They stood tall and straight against the sky, straining heavenward like the great dead men who had built them, and Carl knew he was entering the ruin of a dream.

"Look behind!" Owl shouted. "The Lann are turning back. The old Cities are forbidden to them."

"They are forbidden to us, too," Carl said, spurring his horse forward. "But what have we to lose? Come on, let's find the witches . . ."

VAULT OF THE AGES

POUL ANDERSON

A BERKLEY BOOK
published by
BERKLEY PUBLISHING CORPORATION

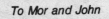
To Mor and John

The Time Capsule

ARCHAEOLOGISTS, studying the past, are handicapped by the fact that relics are usually few and in poor condition. Often, one is not even sure where to look for them. Out of such finds—from tombs, ruined cities, swamps, deserts, and any other place where men of the past have left some trace of themselves—the archaeologist tries to build up a picture of these men's lives and civilizations. But there are great gaps in our knowledge and probably always will be. For instance, we cannot yet read the inscriptions left by the ancient Cretans, and so are in the dark about many features of their high civilization. We know almost nothing of their actual history, and we are not even sure who the people were that finally destroyed them. In like manner, there are many things we would like to know about the Etruscans, Khmers, Mayans, and other important nations and tribes of the past; but we have simply not found enough complete records and relics to have a good picture.

Hundreds of years from now, our own modern civilization may be as remote and mysterious as these cultures. As in this story, where I have laid the scene five hundred years in the future, after our present-day civilization was destroyed by the misuse of the atom bomb, the wise men of that day would be able to learn what we were like from time capsules.

As to what a time capsule is, many definitions could be given, but let us stick to the facts. ''Time capsule'' is a coined name for a container of some kind which is filled with pictures, models, and

other records which give a view as complete as possible of the world
of the time—how the people lived, what they ate and wore and knew
and thought. The container is then buried in a safe place for scientists of the far future to dig up.

The idea of leaving tokens for the future is not entirely new. Such
inscriptions as the great one on the Rock of Behistun, in Asia Minor,
were made so that all men to come would know of the king who had
ordered it. When a Chinese emperor in the third century B.C. tried to
destroy certain texts, scholars hid copies in the hope that later
generations would find them. This hope was realized, and so such
writings as the Confucian Willow Books were saved for posterity.
However, no such systematic attempts as we are discussing were, to
my knowledge, made before the twentieth century. This is probably
because of the difficulty of reconstructing the past, and because
only since Schliemann's time has there been any real science of
archaeology.

I believe there are only two time capsules in existence—one at
Atlanta, Georgia, and one in New York City, which is the best
known.

This time capsule was made by the Westinghouse Company and
was buried in 1938 on the site of the World's Fair of 1939. It was
meant to be dug up again in five thousand years, in A.D. 6938. A
Book of Record was prepared and 3,650 copies printed on perma-
nent paper with special ink. This Book of Record describes the
contents, the exact location, and the purpose of the time capsule. It
also contains a request that it be translated into new languages as
they appear. However, in case this is not done, the book contains a
carefully worked-out phonetic and linguistic key to the English
language, from which any trained linguist can reconstruct our
tongue. One copy was placed in the time capsule itself; the rest,
distributed to libraries, museums, monasteries, lamaseries, tem-
ples, and other safe places around the world. It is hoped that some
few copies, at least, will last the full five thousand years. Even if
none does, the capsule will probably be found someday, for the site
of New York City will always be of great interest to future archaeologists.

The capsule itself is a torpedo-shaped vessel, seven and one-half
feet long and eight and three-eighths inches in diameter, made of
cupraloy (a very resistant alloy of copper) one inch thick. Inside, it
is lined with pyrex glass and, after being packed and the air pumped

out, it was filled with humid nitrogen to preserve the contents from decay and corrosion. It was lowered fifty feet into the earth through a steel pipe to a base of waterproof concrete. Pitch was poured in around it, then a top layer of concrete, after which the pipe was cut off and pulled out and the hole was filled in. With these precautions it should be safe from vandals such as the grave robbers who destroyed much valuable material in the Egyptian pyramids; and geologists have assured us that in five thousand years the land will not have sunk below the sea. The time capsule should easily last its appointed period.

The shell contains messages to the future from prominent men, a copy of the Book of Record and one of the Bible, and various technical aids to translators. There are numerous articles of common usefulness, pleasure, clothing, and vanity, such as a watch, hats, games, money, seeds, pipe and tobacco pouch, and so on. There are also a magnifier and a viewer for the microfilmed texts and the newsreel. This newsreel is a sound film running about fifteen minutes and showing characteristic or significant events of the year 1938—scenes from military maneuvers and the Sino-Japanese War then taking place, a fashion show, a Presidential address, and so on.

On microfilm, there are a great many texts which are meant to give as complete a picture as possible of the world of 1938. There are photographs of industrial processes and works of art; books and encyclopedic articles describing what we knew and did and thought; some outstanding novels and dramas of the twentieth century; and even comic strips.

The entire capsule is, indeed, a treasure chest of information about our own lives and times, not only the great events and discoveries, but the small details of everyday living.

The one at Atlanta is, as far as I know, quite similar, though it contains more models of machinery, houses, and so forth. Probably more time capsules will be laid down from time to time in the future.

As the repository described in this book is not entirely like these, I have called it a "time vault" instead. It was not meant purely for wise men or scientists, but for the common men of the future, whom the maker foresaw would have sunk back to a barbaric state of life. He wanted them to find and enter the vault easily, and use its contents as a guide to rebuilding civilization. To facilitate this, he put his relics in a large cellar or vault underground, lined with concrete so it would not collapse, and left a door above ground for anyone who wished to enter. He did not microfilm his books, since these people of the future would probably not understand what he had done. Instead, he left them in steel cabinets with close-fitting doors, safe from animals, insects, fire, and damp. He chose books which would be easy to read and understand, as well as more complicated ones when the simple texts had been mastered. And he left plans and models not only of the great machines we now have, such as automobiles and airplanes, but also of things which backward peoples could make for themselves right away—balloons, windmills, schooners, simple blast furnaces, and the like. It was his hope that the people of the future would go on from this to make the more powerful machines of his own time. And he left them also the great works of art, literature, religion, and philosophy, hoping that these would teach men to use the machines wisely.

P. A.

Contents

VAULT OF THE AGES

CHAPTER 1

Warriors of Lann

THE SUN was low, slanting its long light through the forests to north and west, and shadows crept over the rolling green farm lands across which Carl had come riding. He saw the buildings ahead as an outlined darkness against the trees beyond, heard noises of cattle and sheep and a barking dog drift through the quiet, and felt his pony break into a trot as it smelled hay and shelter. A wandering sunset breeze ruffled Carl's long hair. He shaded his eyes against the light and leaned forward in the saddle, eager as his horse. It had been a long day's ride.

The dog came running from the farmyard and danced yammering around him as he neared the house. Carl's hand tightened on the hilt of his sword—watchdogs often attacked on these lonely places and had to be beaten off with the flat of a weapon. This one, however, simply kept barking till the evening rang with echoes.

"You there, Bull! Quiet!"

A man stepped out of the house and the dog ran to him and was still. The man remained in the door, waiting with a spear in his hand. He was big and burly, with gray hair that reached to his shoulders and a beard that flowed over his homespun shirt. Two boys stood behind him with axes in their hands.

Carl, smiling, reined in his pony. "Greetings," he said. "I come alone and in peace, asking a roof for the night."

The farmer lowered his spear and nodded. "Then be welcome and stay with us," he replied formally. "I am John, son of Tom, and a Dalesman."

"And I am Carl, son of Ralph in Dalestown," answered the newcomer. "I thank you for your kindness."

"Ralph—in Dalestown!" John's eyes widened. "Then you must be the son of the Chief."

"Yes, I am," Carl said, swinging out of the saddle.

They stood for a moment looking at him. Carl was sixteen years old, but large and strong for his age, with ruddy brown hair, and sun-tanned face and wide-set brown eyes. He wore the usual clothes of a traveler: leather breeches, dyed wool shirt, short homespun cloak, and moccasins. Sword and dagger were belted at his waist and a round shield hung from his saddle beside a bow and quiver. He had a canteen of water but no other supplies; in the wilderness there was plenty of game, and where men lived, a farmer would always give him food and lodging for the sake of company and news.

"Come," one of the boys said eagerly. "I'll show you to the barn and then we'll eat and talk."

He was the elder of John's two sons, a lean, red-haired, freckle-faced lad of about Carl's age. His brother, who followed them, was perhaps a year younger, short and stout and blond. "I am Tom," said the older boy, "and this is Owl."

"Owl?" asked Carl.

"His real name is Jim," said Tom, "but nobody ever calls him anything but Owl. He looks like one, doesn't he?"

"It is because I am so wise," smiled his brother.

The farm buildings were long and low, made from rough-hewn timbers chinked with clay and moss. Within the barn there were several horses and cows, and a twilight thick with the rich smell of animals and hay. Tom led Carl's pony to a vacant stall while Owl brought water.

"You have a big place here," said Carl. "I wouldn't have thought it. You live right on the edge of the great forest and the border of the Dales."

"Why shouldn't we have a good farm?" asked Tom.

"Well—a place like this would tempt raiders, I should think."

"There are none," said Owl. "The woods-runners around here were driven away a hundred years ago. You should know that."

"I do," answered Carl gravely. "But there are worse than woods-runners—and they're on their way."

"You mean the Lann." Tom's voice grew flat. "We can speak of them later."

Carl shrugged, but there was a sudden bleakness in him. It had been this way all the time, everywhere he went. So few would believe the story, so few could rise above the narrowness of their lives and see that the Dales faced a threat beyond their worst dreams.

He clamped his mouth shut and helped care for the pony. When the three boys came out, the sun had set and twilight stole from the east, rising like mist between the high trees. They walked across the muddy yard toward the cheerful fire-glow of the house.

The long room inside was bounded by curtained beds at one end and a stone hearth at the other. John's wife, a tall woman in the long-skirted dress of the Dales, was cooking supper there. She smiled at Carl and greeted him in a friendly way, but he saw the worry in her face and knew that she was not altogether deaf to the stories of the Lann. Besides John, who sat at the plank-table smoking a corncob pipe, there were two young men who were introduced to Carl as Arn and Samwell, workers on the farm.

It was a handsome and comfortable house, thought Carl, letting his eyes travel around it. The soft light of home-dipped tallow candles fell on skin rugs, on a loom with a rich, half-woven tapestry stretched across it, on pots and bowls of baked clay and hammered copper. It slanted over weapons racked against one wall and the weapons threw back the light in a fierce iron blink, deflecting it off a faded picture of a man, one of the marvelous works which must have been handed down since the Day of Doom. And all this could go up in flame when the Lann arrived!

The Dalesmen did not think it polite to talk of serious matters before a guest had been fed, so they spoke of weather and animals and neighborhood gossip. Unreal, thought Carl, swallowing his impatience. They sat and gabbled about rain and crops when the storm of conquest even then roared down from the north. The food, when at last it was served, was tasteless in his mouth.

After the dishes had been cleared off and the fire built up against the cool dampness of early summer night, John gave him a shrewd glance across the table. A wavering red light danced through the room, weaving a pattern of huge rippling shadows in the corners from which Arn looked superstitiously away. The farmer's eyes gleamed out of a face that was half in darkness, and he puffed a blue cloud of smoke into the air.

"And how are things in Dalestown, Carl?" he asked.

This was the time to speak! "The men are gathering," answered Carl, choosing his words slowly, with care. "In the east and west and south the Dalesmen have heard the war-word of their Chief and are sending their fighting men to join him. Dalestown has grown noisy with men and weapons. Only from this part of our northern lands have no men yet come." He raised his eyebrows. "You will march soon, of course?"

"We will not march at all," said John calmly. "The men of the northern Dales are staying at home."

"But—" Carl checked his words. After all, this was no surprise; Ralph's messengers had brought back the answer of these land-holders already. Finally he said slowly, "But you are in the very path of the invaders."

"Perhaps," replied John. "And in that case, should we abandon our homes to their plundering, leave our women and children and animals unshielded while all our warriors are at Dalestown?"

"My father," said Carl desperately, "is gathering all the men of the tribe together so he can have an army of proper size with which to meet these Lann and drive them back where they came from. Do you few border dwellers expect to stop the enemy alone?"

"We stood off the woods-runners long ago," said John. "I don't think the Lann will be any worse."

"But they are!" cried the boy. "We know!"

John raised his brows. "And what do you know of the Lann? I thought there was no traffic northward."

"Very little," said Carl. "We get what we need for ourselves in the Dales, and our traders carry what extra we have south to get fruits and tobacco or east for fish and salt. Still, travelers have gone into the cold lands from time to time, and they have told us that the tribes living there are poor and backward, but very fierce. Someone brought word back a couple of years ago that these tribes had united under one Chief and were talking of coming south."

"Why should they do that?" asked Tom. "It's a long way from their homes to ours."

"We live better," said Carl. "Our land is rich, our forests are full of game and timber, our ancient cities yield so much metal that we can even trade it with other people—oh, I can see where these northerners, these Lann as they call themselves, would envy us. Their own scouts and explorers have visited us now and then, you know.''

He ran a hand through his hair. ''Also,'' he went on, ''this is a matter which I do not understand very well, but some say the world is getting colder. Old men all tell how the summers were warmer and the winters shorter in their youth, that their grandfathers had told them things were still better. Old Donn, the High Doctor at Dalestown, who keeps the ancient wisdom, says that the wise men before the Doom knew of such changes too. Anyway,'' he finished lamely, ''if the weather really is getting colder and stormier, it would strike the north first and hardest. They have had several bitter years and thin harvests, my father's spies have told, and are themselves harried by desperate raiders from still farther north. So all in all, it is easy to see that the Chief of the united Lann may want to lead a host which can conquer the south and take its lands.''

''That would take a great army,'' said Owl.

''It is a great army,'' said Carl grimly.

''But why should they fall on us?'' asked John. ''There are weaker tribes, easier prey.''

''I don't know,'' said Carl, ''but my father thinks it's just because we Dalesmen are the largest and strongest of the tribes that they want to overrun us first. Once we are beaten, our neighbors will have no chance.'' He scowled. ''Even so, those other tribes won't join with us. They're afraid to stir up the anger of the Lann. We stand alone.''

''And where is this northern army?'' asked John.

''I don't know,'' said Carl. ''Nobody does. They could be anywhere in the great hills and forests to the north, and will move almost as fast as any scout of ours could bring word of their coming. I suppose they're scattered through the woods, so they can live off the country better, and will join forces again when they come out into the farm lands. There've been fights elsewhere in the northern marches between some of their advance guards and men of ours, so they must be near.''

''But no one can tell how near, eh?'' John knocked out his pipe. A tiny coal glowed in the ashes for a moment and then went out like a closing eye. ''I thought so. You see, Carl, it isn't at all sure that the

Lann will come out of the woods just hereabouts, or if they do that it will be a force too big for us to handle, or even if it's their whole army that it will waste time attacking the gathered warriors of this neighborhood. So all in all, we men of this district voted to stay at home and defend our own hearth-fires."

"It was your right under the law," admitted Carl gloomily, "but a divided tribe is a weak tribe."

He sat for a while in a stillness broken only by the crackling of the fire and the whisper of the loom where John's wife worked. Somewhere outside, a wild dog howled, and Bull stirred where he lay on a deerskin and snarled an answer.

"It isn't so bad," said John kindly. "We'll win out. There may not even be a war." He smiled. "Besides, lad, I don't think you're here as Ralph's messenger to us border men."

"No," said Carl, brightening in spite of himself. "I'm really heading north to the City."

"The City!" whispered Owl, and a stir of awe ran about the room. John's eyes narrowed, Tom leaned forward with his thin, sharp face drawn tight, Arn and Samwell looked at each other, and the woman at the loom stopped her weaving for a startled instant.

"It isn't far from here, is it?" asked Carl.

"Only about a day's ride," said Tom slowly. "But none of us have ever been there. It's taboo."

"Not completely," Carl told him. "The Chief of a tribe can send men to bargain with the witch-men smiths there. That's me."

"You're after iron weapons, I suppose?"

"Yes. Every Dalesman has his own war tools, of course, but we need things like catapults and horse armor to fight the Lann. I'm supposed to get them from the smiths in return for the usual payment—meat, salt, cloth, furs, you know."

A wild dog howled again, closer this time. The woods were full of such packs, descendants, it was said, of tame animals which had run loose when the Doom scattered men. They were among the most dangerous beasts these days. Arn grunted, took a brand from the fire for light, and went out with Samwell to check the sheepfold.

Carl sat letting his mind run over what he knew of the City. He had never been there, and his being sent on this errand was a proud sign that the son of the Chief was becoming a man.

Once there stood towns and villages even in this region of the

Allegheny Mountains. They had been abandoned during the Doom or shortly thereafter and had moldered to ruin. After early smiths had plundered all the metal in them, they had been left for the wind and the forests to bury, and today their fragments, thought to be haunted, were left alone by the tribes. As the other ancient metal—from houses, rusted machines, and the mysterious old railroad tracks—was used up, men looked toward the vaster ruins of the old cities.

But by that time, taboos had grown up. Early explorers venturing into some of the empty metropolises—those which had been wrecked and burned by the terrible fury from the air which was the Doom—had often died of lingering sickness, and many thought that the ''glowing death'' was the sign of godly anger. So today the ruins, like other ancient works, were forbidden to tribesmen.

Still, metal was needed. A hundred years, or perhaps two hundred, after the Doom, little groups of outcasts had drifted into the cities and lived there. Not belonging to any of the great tribes, they had not been kept from going; but today they were shunned and feared as witch-men, in spite of being usually a timid and unwarlike folk. It was they who salvaged steel and copper from the huge ruined buildings, sometimes forging it themselves into tools and weapons, sometimes selling the metal as it was. Tribesmen were allowed to come and buy from them, providing that afterward a Doctor said magic over the things to take the curse off.

In all this region, only one such city remained—*the* City. No one remembered its name today. It lay some distance north of the Dalesmen's territory, screened by the hills and forests which reached farther than anyone had ever traveled. Carl had long been eager to visit it, but this was the first time Ralph had allowed him.

He spoke again, his words seeming loud in the quietness: ''I need a guide. Will anyone come with me?''

John shook his head. ''The City is a bad place.''

''I do not think so,'' said Carl. ''It was a great and glorious world before the Doom smashed everything. The ancient people were wiser men than we. Why should their works be evil?''

It was a new thought, and they sat turning it carefully over in their minds. ''Taboo,'' said John at last.

''I have leave to go there,'' answered Carl.

Tom leaned forward, his eyes alight, shivering a little. "Yes—Father, I can guide him!" he said.

"You?"

"And I," said Owl. "It's a shame, our living a day's ride from the City and never having seen it."

"We'll be back in two days," cried Tom.

"The Lann—" muttered John.

"You said they were nowhere near," grinned Owl.

"But—"

"It is the tribe which asks you," said Carl urgently. "All the Dalesmen need those weapons."

John argued for a long time, but when Carl went to bed he knew he had won.

They were up with sunrise, Owl groaning and complaining at the earliness of it. "He's like that," smiled Tom. "He won't be really awake till after breakfast."

Carl rubbed his eyes, yawning. "I know how he feels."

They went out in a cool gray mist and helped with the morning's work. When they came back to the house, leading saddled horses, breakfast was waiting, and Carl ate as hungrily as his new friends.

John's wife, Mary, hovered over the boys. "Be careful," she whispered. "Be careful, Tom, Jim, and—oh, come back to us!"

"Yes," rumbled John in his beard. "I shouldn't let you go, but—the gods go with you." His rough hand brushed their shoulders and he turned away, blinking.

The three were too eager to be off to pay much attention. It seemed a long time to Carl before he was riding into the woods, but the mist was still not quite off the ground and dew was shining in the grass.

"I know the way," said Tom, "even if I've never been there myself. We follow this trail till we get to a brook, then it's due north across country to one of the old roads, and that'll take us straight in."

"If it's that easy," said Carl, "I don't need a guide."

"Oh, yes, you do," said Owl. "At least, I need the trip."

They rode single file down a narrow path. Before long, the forest had closed in on them, brush and fern and high, sun-dappled trees, a red squirrel streaking up a mossy trunk, chatter of birds and murmur of running water—but they were alone, there were no others anywhere, and the great stillness lay like a cloak over all the lesser noises. Carl relaxed in the saddle, listening with half an ear to the excited talk of Tom and Owl, aware of the plod of hoofs and the squeak of leather and the jingle of metal, his nostrils sensing a thousand smells of green growing life. It was a good land here, a broad, fair land of green fields and tall forests and strong people— and by all the gods, the Dalesmen meant to keep it!

"I know why Father let us go with you," said Tom. "He is upset about our neighborhood not sending men to Dalestown. He thinks it's still the wisest thing we're doing, but he doesn't really like it."

"Nobody likes war," said Carl shortly.

"I think the Lann must," said Owl. "Otherwise, why are they making it against us? We never harmed them."

Carl didn't answer. Indeed, he thought, he was not at all sure of why things were happening or of what really was going on. The world, big and secret, held more in it than the tribes with their unchanging life or the Doctors with their narrow wisdom thought.

They rode on, and the sun climbed in the sky and the forest slid away behind them and still loomed ahead. The trail faded out near a cold running brook which they forded, and beyond that, the hills climbed steeply, with many open meadows between the trees. They rested at noon, eating the dried meat which John's sons had taken along, and then mounted again and rode farther.

The attack came near midafternoon. Carl was riding in the lead, pushing a way through a dense part of the forest, lost in his own thoughts. Their own passage was so noisy that the boys did not hear anything else, and the sudden yell came like a thunderbolt.

Carl whipped out his sword and dug heels into his pony's ribs in one unthinking motion. The arrow hummed past his cheek and stuck into a tree. He saw the man who rose out of ambush before him and hewed wildly even as the stranger's ax chopped at his leg.

Metal clanged on metal, flaming in a single long sunbeam. The man yelled again, and others came out of the brush and dropped from the limbs of trees. Carl reined in his horse, it reared back and its hoofs slashed at the first attacker. He stumbled backward to escape, and Carl bent low in the saddle and burst into a gallop.

"This way!" he yelled. "This way, after me! We've got to get clear! It's the Lann!"

CHAPTER 2

The Lost City

BRANCHES whipped across his face, and Carl flung up an arm to shield his eyes. Forward—a wild scrambling as the Lann warriors broke before his charge—out and away! He burst from the woods into the long grass of a sunlit meadow. Two arrows whistled after him; one grazed his neck, humming like an angry bee. Turning in the saddle, he saw Tom and Owl riding close behind him and the enemy running into the open.

A horseman topped the crest of the hill to his right, light flashing off his iron helmet. If they had cavalry to pursue—Carl set his teeth and clucked to his pony. Fast, fast—the way back was cut off, they had to go forward.

Up a long slope, down into a gulch below, with the horses slipping and stumbling on loose earth, around a thicket and through a brier-patch that clawed at living flesh. Carl risked another glance behind and saw half a dozen armed men on the small shaggy horses of the north, galloping in an easy chase. Their mounts were fresh, thought the boy; they need only run down their wearied prey and after that, the end—or capture, which could be worse than death.

The long-legged steeds of John's sons drew up on either side of Carl. Tom was bent low, his face white and set; Owl was riding easily, his lips even now curled in a half-smile. Leaning over, the younger boy shouted to Carl, ''Looks like we'll get there sooner than we thought!''

11

"The City?" cried his brother.

"Where else?" panted Carl. "Maybe the witches will help us."

It was a forlorn hope. The smith-folk knew they existed only on sufferance and on the tribesmen's unwillingness to enter the Cities, so they would never risk the anger of anyone by mixing into the quarrels of others. But—what else was there for the hunted to do?

Ride, ride, ride! The wind roared in Carl's ears, whipping his hair and cloak behind him, the land seemed to blur past, the fury of speed stung his eyes with tears. Already his horse was breathing heavily, sweating and foaming. How much longer could it go on?

The Lann were out of sight behind the rolling hills, but they would follow. Even as he guided his mount over the rough ground and wondered how long he would still be alive, Carl was thinking back over what he had seen. Except for one or two prisoners taken in border skirmishes, he had never met a Lann warrior before, and the image of his pursuers was sharp in his mind.

The northerners were of the same race as the Dalesmen and the other Allegheny tribes, though a life of hardships had made them a little shorter and stockier; and their language was almost the same, easily understood. Even their clothing was much like that of the Dales, with more fur and leather used. But the fighting men all seemed to have breastplates of toughened hide painted in harsh colors, their swords were often curved instead of straight, and they used a shorter, heavier bow. It was said that they fought in a tighter and better arranged formation than the Dalesmen, who were peaceful folk and had no real art of war.

Faintly to Carl's ears, above the rush of wind and murmur of grass and thudding of hoofs, there came the sound of a blown horn, wailing and hooting between the empty hills. A signal. Were the Lann calling to others? Would there be a whole army chasing three hapless boys? A gulp of despair rose in Carl's throat. He choked it down and urged his pony to another effort.

Up a slanting, crumbling bluff. From its heights, Carl saw the enemy, more of them now, perhaps twenty. They had been joined by others, and where in all the reaching world was there shelter from them?

As he plunged down the hill beyond, Carl saw a dull, white gleam through a screen of trees. A river—no, it was no stream, no trail— nothing! Straight as a hurled spear it ran northward, and Tom let out a yell as he saw it.

"The road!" he shouted. "The road to the City!"

Of course, thought Carl. He had seen the broken remnants of ancient highways, split by the ages, most of the blocks taken away by men for building material. This one had not been disturbed, and it ran toward their goal.

They came out on the road and its hard surface rang hollowly under the hoofs. "Ride on it!" said Owl. "It's a fast and easy way—"

"Also for the Lann," said Tom bleakly. "But come."

The frost and creeping roots of centuries had been cruel to the highway, Carl saw. Its great stony sections lay riven and cracked, tilted at crazy angles and often overgrown with brush. But still it was there, and it was straight and almost level. Ride, ride, ride!

As they sped on their way, he noticed low grassy mounds on either side of the road. Under those, he knew, were buried the decayed ruins of ancient houses. Bold men sometimes defied taboo and dug about in such hills, finding the broken pieces of things incomprehensible to them. Even now, racing for his life, Carl could not help a shudder, and from the corner of an eye he saw Tom fingering a lucky charm about his neck.

The mounds grew larger and closer together as the boys galloped north. Here and there a shattered fragment of worked stone, a few bricks, or a gleaming splinter of glass thrust out of the green overgrowth. The drumbeats of the hoofs rolled and echoed between those solemnly looming graves as if the dead woke up and cried in protest.

"The Lann—coming—"

Turning at Owl's voice, Carl saw the tiny figures of the enemy horsemen far behind, galloping down the highway with the westering sun flashing off their spears and helmets. Then Tom's cry jerked his head forward again.

"The City!"

They were riding between two high mounds which over-shadowed the road and blocked off the view ahead. As they burst out from between these, their goal lay open to them.

The City—the ancient City!

Even then, Carl felt the awe and the sadness which lay over that dead titan. It sprawled farther away on every side than he could see, and it was toppled to ruin and waste. The buildings on this edge were little more than heaps of brick covered with vines and bush and young trees, and here and there a wall still stood erect under the creepers. The forest had crept in, blanketing the great old works in green, slowly and patiently gnawing them down; and wind and rain and frost had over the centuries brought them toppling; and wild beasts laired in the wreck and prowled the hollow streets.

But far, far down, the towers, which had been the City's pride, gleamed in the long, low sunrays. Even from this distance, Carl could see that they were gutted. Many of the walls had fallen, leaving a rusted steel skeleton; the windows were empty and the blowing air wandered between dusty rooms—yet they stood, tall and straight against the evening sky, straining heavenward like the great dead men who had wrought them, and Carl knew that he was entering the ruin of a dream.

"The Lann—Tom, Carl, look behind! The Lann!"

They had reined in their horses between the two sentinel mounds and were milling in confusion. Their shouts drifted faintly down the sunset breeze to the boys sitting on their horses under the somber walls of a roofless building.

"Taboo!" shouted Owl gleefully. "The old Cities are forbidden to them too. They don't dare enter!"

Carl drew a long, shuddering breath, and it was as if life and hope flowed back into him with it. He laughed aloud, there in the stillness of the lost city.

"But—" Tom looked nervously around him. "We're breaking the taboo ourselves."

Purpose returned to Carl. He straightened his weary shoulders and looked boldly ahead. "What have we to lose?" he asked. "Come on, let's find the witches."

The tired, sweating horses walked slowly down a street which was overgrown with grass and creepers. The echoes rang loud in that great stillness. A family of swallows dipped and wheeled overhead, swift and lovely against the golden sunset sky. This could not be such a terrible place, thought Carl.

It had long been his idea that the tribes and the Doctors were wrong in forbidding the ancient works. Perhaps they had, as was said, brought the Doom on mankind—but they had so much power for good in them that he felt they could start today's unchanging life back upward toward the heights the ancestors had reached. Now, as he rode through the shadows and the tall, sad remnants, the belief was strengthened in him.

"Halt! Halt!"

The voice was shrill in Carl's ears. He clapped one hand to his sword and reined in before the score of men who had come from around a wall and stood barring the road. The witch-folk!

They did not seem like the uncanny beings of whispered midnight stories. They were men even as those in the Dales—rather small and skinny men too, who handled their weapons awkwardly and seemed as shy as Tom and Owl had suddenly become. Most of them were very dark-skinned. They must have blood of the black tribes which lived in the southlands, as well as the white of the Alleghenys and the north. Unlike the other tribes, they wore tunics and kilts, and their hair was cut short.

One of them stepped out of the line and raised a thin hand. He was taller than his fellows, and old, with a white beard flowing from his wrinkled face, and a long fur-trimmed cloak wrapped his gaunt body. There was something in his deep-set blue eyes which made Carl like him even at first glance.

"You may not come in here," said the old man. "It is forbidden."

"By our own tribes, not by your laws," said Carl. "And even our own laws let a man save his life. There are foemen from the north hunting us. If we go out now, they will kill us."

"Go!" cried a witch-man. His voice trembled. "We dare not have anything to do with the wars of the tribes."

Carl grinned. "If you send us out," he said, "you are taking the northern part against the Dalesmen." Turning to the old man: "Sir, we come as your guests."

"Then you can stay," decided the witch-man at once. "For a while, at least. We of the City know what a host must do as well as you in the Dales."

"But—" His followers began to murmur, and he turned angrily on them.

"I say these lads stay!" he snapped, and one by one the threatening spears were lowered.

"Thank you, sir," said Carl. Then he gave the names of himself and his companions, and told their errand.

"The son of Ralph, eh?" The old witch-man looked keenly at the boy. "I remember Ralph when he came here once. A strong man, and wiser than most. Welcome, Carl. I am Ronwy, Chief of the City folk."

Carl dismounted, and they shook hands. "We will give you food and shelter," said Ronwy. "But as for making weapons for you—that I cannot promise. The Chief of the city, like the Chief of a tribe, cannot do whatever he wishes; he is bound by law and the vote of his people. I must take this up with the others in council." His blue glance was shrewd. "And even if we made your engines for you, how would you get them past the Lann? We know they're all around this neighborhood."

Carl gulped back his sudden dismay and followed Ronwy, leading his weary horse down the streets. The witch-men grumbled among themselves and went their separate ways.

After a mile or so of walking in silence, the boys and their guide came to the outskirts of the section where the towers were. Here the buildings were taller and stronger than near the edge, and had stood the years of weathering better. Brush had been cleared away, rooms repaired and filled with household goods, new doors put on empty frames and the broken windows covered with thin-scraped parchment—this was the place where the witch-folk lived. They moved about on their daily errands, men and women and children walking between the enormous walls, firelight and the smell of cooking food coming from the houses, a banjo twanging somewhere in the dusk, the faint clang of a hammer from the open door of a smithy.

"They aren't so terrible," whispered Owl. "They're people just like us—not very many of them, either. I don't see any devils or ghosts."

"Have the old stories lied?" wondered Tom.

"Maybe," said Carl. He was too unsure of his own thoughts to go on.

Ronwy led them to his own dwelling, a long room with high ceilings on the first story of an ancient tower. There was a marble floor, Carl saw wonderingly, and some of the old dishes and glasses and metal ornaments stood on the crude wooden tables of this age. Had the world really sunk so far from greatness?

Ronwy lit candles, chasing the gloom back into the corners, and motioned them to chairs. "Be seated," he said. "My servants will take care of your horses and bring food shortly. I'm glad of your company. My wife is long dead and my sons are grown men and it's lonesome here. You must tell me what is going on in the Dales."

Tom shivered in the evening chill and Ronwy began to stoke the fireplace. It had been built in later days, with the chimney going up through a hole in the cracked ceiling. "In the ancient time," said the Chief, "there was always warmth in here, without fire; and if you wanted light, it came from little glass balls which only had to be touched."

Carl looked at the table beside his chair. A book lay on it, and he picked it up and leafed through the yellowed pages with awe in him.

"Do you know what that is?" asked Ronwy.

"It's called a book," said Carl. "The High Doctor in Dalestown has a few."

"Can you read?"

"Yes, sir, and write too. I'm the Chief's son, so I had to learn. We sometimes send letters—" Carl puzzled over the words before him. "But this doesn't make sense!"

"It's a physics text," answered Ronwy. "It explains—well— how the ancients did some of their magic." He smiled sadly. "I'm afraid it doesn't mean much to me either."

A serving-woman brought dishes of food and the boys attacked it hungrily. Afterward they sat and talked of many things until Ronwy showed them to bed.

He liked the City, Carl decided as he lay waiting for sleep to come. It was hard to believe in this quiet place that war and death waited outside. But he remembered grimly that the Lann had hunted him to the very edge of the tabooed zone. The witch-folk wouldn't let him stay long here, in spite of Ronwy—and the Lann swords would be waiting, sharp and hungry, for him to come out again.

CHAPTER 3

Wisdom of the Ancients

IN THE morning, at breakfast, Ronwy told the boys: "I will gather the men of the City in council today and try to get them to vote for making the things you need. These northern invaders are a savage people, and the Dalesmen have always been our friends." His smile was a little bitter. "Or as nearly our friends as we outcasts have."

"Where is the meeting held?" asked Tom.

"In the great hall down the street," said Ronwy. "But by our law, no outsiders may attend such councils, so you might as well explore the City today. If you aren't afraid of ghosts and devils—and I, in all my life here, have never met any—you should be interested."

"The City!" Carl's heart thudded with sudden excitement. The City, the City, the wonderful magic City—*he* would be roaming through it!

"Be careful, though," said Ronwy. "There are many old pits and other dangerous places hidden by brush and rubble. Snakes are not unknown either. I will see you here again in the evening."

Taking some bread and meat along for lunch, Carl and his friends wandered outside and down the streets. Whatever fear they had was soon lost in the marvel of it all; but a great awe, tinged with the sorrow of a world's loss, took its place.

The witch-folk were about their daily business, sullenly ignoring the strangers. Women cooked and spun and tended babies. Children scrambled through empty houses and over great heaps of rubble, or sat listening to the words of an old teacher sitting under a tree. Men were doing their various tasks. Some worked in the little gardens planted in open spaces, some were in smithies and carpenter shops, some drove wagonloads of goods down wide avenues which must have carried more traffic in the old days than Carl could imagine. The boy was struck afresh by the pitiful smallness of this life, huddled in the vast wreck of its godlike ancestors, puzzling dimly over things it could never understand—much less rebuild. He sighed.

A great gong boomed solemnly down the air, echoing from wall to wall. It was Ronwy's first summons, telling the witch-men that a council would meet in the afternoon.

"Look, Carl. Look up there!"

The Chief's son craned his neck as Owl pointed. Up the sheer wall of an ancient tower, up, up, *up,* unbelievably far up. The stories said these buildings had been called skyscrapers, and indeed, thought Carl wildly, their heights seemed to storm the heavens.

The scarred brick facing was gone after the first few stories, and only a skeleton of giant rust-red girders was left above, a dark net of emptiness through which the wind piped its mournful song. Clambering around on those mighty ribs were the tiny forms of men. The sound of their hammers and chisels drifted faintly down to the boys, and now and then the flame of a crude blowtorch would wink like a star caught in the steel net. The heavy ropes of a block and tackle reached from the heights down to the weed-grown street.

"What are they doing?" whispered Tom.

"They're tearing it down," said Carl, very softly. "Piece by piece, they're ripping out the steel to sell to the tribes." A shivering wind rippled about his words and blew them down the hollow canyon of the avenue.

There was a huge sadness in it—the little men of today, gnawing apart the mighty works they no longer understood. In a few hundred years, or a few thousand, what did it matter? Nothing would be left, nothing but rubble and waving grass and the wild dogs howling where men had once lived.

Sorrow wrestled in Carl with a slowly gathering anger. It was wrong, it was wrong. The ancient wisdom was *not* accursed! Men should be trying to learn it and use it to rebuild—not let time and the witch-folk eat it away. Already a priceless heritage was gone; if this greed and ignorance were not halted, nothing would be left for the future.

His gloom deepened as the three prowled further. So little remained. The buildings were gutted long ago. Nothing remained but empty shells and the clumsy things of today's dwellers. Beyond this central part where the people lived, everything had simply been stripped of metal and left to crumble. The forest had grown far into the town.

Owl would not be stopped from climbing several stories up one of the towers, and Tom and Carl followed him. From that windy height they could look miles over the dead City and the hills and woods beyond. To the north a broad river ran through the toppled ruin of a great bridge. Today, thought Carl bleakly, they had only a couple of wooden scows for getting over. He looked south too, after some sign of the Lann, but could see only waving, sunlit green of trees. They were waiting, though. They were waiting.

It was nearly noon when the boys found the vault which was to mean so much to them. They were exploring the southern edge of the inhabited section, skirting a wall of bush and young trees that screened off the long low sides of caved-in buildings, when Tom pointed and cried, "What's that?"

Carl approached the thing gingerly, afraid in spite of himself. A pole stuck in the ground bore the skull of a horse—a common sign to keep off evil spirts. Beyond this were the two sides of a house otherwise fallen to heaps of brick and glass. At the rear of those parallel walls was a curious gray object like nothing he had seen before.

"It's magic," said Tom, holding fast to his lucky charm. "The witches put up that sign because they're afraid of whatever it is."

"Ronwy said there weren't any ghosts here," replied Owl stanchly. "He ought to know."

Carl stood for a moment thinking. In spite of having no great faith in the old stories of evil, he could not keep his heart from thumping. The thing brooding there in the hot, white sunlight was of the unknown. But—it was that fear which had kept men from learning what their ancestors had to teach. "Come on," he said swiftly, before he could have time to get really frightened. "Let's go see."

"Maybe—" Tom licked his lips, then tossed his red head. "All right! I'm not scared either."

"Not much, anyway," said Owl.

They moved carefully through the grass-grown mounds of rubble, poking ahead with Tom's spear in case of snakes, until they were at the rear of the old house. Then they stood for a long time staring at the mystery.

It was a concrete block, about ten feet square and seven feet high, with a door of age-eaten bronze in the front. There were letters engraved in the gray cement above the door, and Carl spelled them slowly out:

TIME VAULT

"What's a vault?" asked Tom.

"It's a place where you keep things," said Carl.

"But you can't keep time," said Owl. "Time's not a thing. It's a—well—it's *time*. Days and years."

"That's a very strong magic," said Tom, his voice trembling a little. "Or else whoever made this was crazy. Let's go."

"I wonder—that door—" Carl pushed against the heavy green metal. It creaked slowly open, and he saw concrete steps leading down into a great darkness.

"You boys! Get away!"

The boys whirled, and saw a witch-man standing just outside the pole. He held a drawn bow in his hands, the arrow pointing at them, and his angry face made it plain that he meant business.

"Come out!" he shouted. "It's forbidden!"

Carl and his friends scrambled back, secretly a little glad to be ordered from the vault. "I'm sorry," said Carl. "We didn't know."

"If you weren't guests, I'd kill you," said the witch-man. "That place is taboo. It's full of black magic."

"How do you know, if you can't go in?" asked Owl impudently.

"People have been in there," spat the man. "It's full of machines and books and things. The same black magic that brought the Doom. We don't want it to get loose again."

He watched them go down the street and muttered charms against the devils in the vault.

"I'm sorry," said Ronwy, when the boys returned to his house in the evening. "My folk are afraid to deal with anyone till they see how this war with the Lann comes out. I couldn't convince them otherwise. And they said you could stay here only three more nights. If the enemy hasn't given up by then, you'll have to try sneaking past them."

Carl nodded absently, too full of the day's discoveries to think of his own danger right away. He had to talk to someone, and Ronwy's wise blue gaze invited faith.

Carl spilled out the story of what he had seen and thought, and Ronwy tugged his white beard and smiled sadly.

"I've spent my life reading the old histories and other books we've found, and thinking about them," he said. "I believe I know what the Doom really was."

"There was a war," said Tom eagerly.

"Yes. The tribes—they called them nations—were much bigger then. This whole land, farther than any man has traveled today, was owned by one nation called America, and there were other lands too—some of them even across the sea. They had many wars and were very cruel, destroying whole cities from the air and laying the country waste. Finally, one great war ruined so many cities and machines, and killed so many people, that things couldn't go on. There was plague and famine. By that time, too, so much of the land had been used up that people couldn't go back to a simple life in the country, so many of them starved to death; and the others fought over what was left, bringing themselves still lower. Finally only a few remained and the land could feed them, so things got better after a while. But there were those who believed the old machines and powers had brought this evil to pass. If men hadn't had machines that ran over the ground, and sailed, and flew, and destroyed, they wouldn't have been able to hurt each other so much. These people convinced the others that the old wisdom—science, they called it— was bad and should be forbidden. Since very few were left who even understood science, it was easy to kill them or make them keep still.

"That was about five hundred years ago. Since then, the forests and the soil have come back and more people can live off the land than could right after the Doom. We have rebuilt until we live as you see today. But because of the taboos and the fear, we have not gone on to rebuild all that our ancestors had."

Carl nodded slowly. "I thought it was something like that," he said.

"But maybe the taboos are right," said Tom. "If it weren't for the—the science, there couldn't have been the Doom and all the suffering."

"Neither could there have been many good things," answered Ronwy. "The ancients were not afraid of smallpox and the coughing sickness and other diseases which plague us today, because they had conquered them through science. Men lived in a plenty we cannot imagine today, and they had so much to do and see and think about that they were like gods. They lived longer and happier lives than we. Drought in one place did not mean that the people starved, for they could bring food from somewhere else in the world. The cold weather which has driven the Lann south against the Dales would not have mattered to them. Oh, there was so much they did, and so much they were about to do. . . .

"Yes, they were cruel and foolish and brought the Doom on themselves. But why can we not learn from their mistakes? Why can we not use their science to live as they did, and at the same time be kinder and wiser? The world today is a world of want, and therefore a world of war; but we could build a future in which there was no hunger, no fear, no battle against man and nature. Think it over, boys! Think it over!"

Carl woke instantly at the touch on his shoulder and sat up in bed. Gloom of night filled the chamber, but he could dimly see the City Chief's tall form bending over him.

"What is it?" he breathed, fumbling for the dagger he kept under his pillow.

"Uh—ugh—*whoof!*" Tom and Owl stirred in the double bed they shared and sat up, blinking into the night. Carl saw them as deeper shadows in the slowly stirring murk.

"Carl," whispered Ronwy. "Listen to me, Carl. There isn't much time."

"Yes, yes, what is it?" The boy swung out of the blankets, feeling the floor cold under his bare feet.

"I have talked to you, and I think you believe as I," came the rapid murmur out of the darkness. "About the old science, and the need—the very desperate need—of today's world for a rebirth of knowledge. No one else will listen. I've been alone with my dreams, all my life. But you are son of the Chief of the greatest tribe in these lands. Someday, if the Dalesmen are not conquered, you will be their Chief yourself and able to do much.

"I want to show you the time vault. Now, while the City sleeps. Will you come with me?"

Strangely unafraid, strangely calm and steady except for the high pulse within him, Carl slipped on trousers and sword belt. Tom and Owl readied themselves at his back; there was the faintest chatter of teeth, but they would follow him even into the lair of the Doom, and he felt warm at the knowledge. Noiseless on bare feet, the three boys slipped out after Ronwy.

In the moonless dark, the City was a place of looming shadows, streets like tunnels of night, a ghostly breeze and the tiny patter of a hurrying rat. A pair of bats swooped blackly against the dim glow of the Milky Way, and a wild dog howled far off in the woods. Ghostly, flitting through the enormous night silence and the small fearful noises below a wheeling sky, the four humans made their way to the forbidden place.

Tom and Owl and even Carl shivered when they stood under the dim white skull that marked it, but Ronwy drew a long breath. "No one lives near by," he said. "We can talk now."

As they groped carefully toward the vault, he went on: "As Chief, I do have power to go here whenever I wish, and I have spent long times studying the marvels within. But my people won't let me remove anything from it. They're afraid. All the world is afraid. Man's greatest devil is fear."

The door still gaped open on unknown blacknesses. Ronwy struck flint and steel to light a candle he bore. "Follow me," he said. The yellow glow picked his face out of night, old and calm and immensely comforting. "I have entered often. There is no magic, no Doom—nothing to be afraid of—only wonder and mystery."

They went down the steps. At the bottom, Ronwy lifted his candle high and Carl saw that the vault was a great underground chamber lined with concrete, reaching farther into shadowy distance than he could see. He stood unmoving, caught up in the marvel of it.

Steel cabinets stretched along the sides. Long benches held models protected under glass covers: cunningly wrought models of engines whose purpose Carl could not imagine, their metal catching the light in a dull shimmer. Full-size things of steel and copper and glass, shapes such as he had never dreamed, quietly waited for a man who understood. And there were books—books, everywhere books, shelf after glassed-in shelf of books from floor to ceiling—

"Come here," said Ronwy.

Carl followed him over to a wall on which there was a bronze plaque. The boy's lips moved as he slowly puzzled out what was engraved thereon.

TO YOU WHO COME AFTER: THE WORLD IS ON THE EDGE OF THE FINAL WAR, THE WAR WHICH I THINK WILL DESTROY ALL CIVILIZATION AND HURL MAN, IF MAN SURVIVES, BACK TO SAVAGERY AND IGNORANCE. IT WILL TAKE LONG TO REGAIN WHAT IS LOST. PERHAPS IT WILL NEVER BE DONE. BUT I MUST DO WHAT I CAN TO SAVE THE KNOWLEDGE WHICH IS SO GREAT AND GOOD. IT IS MEN WHO ARE EVIL AND MISUSE THEIR POWERS; THEIR KNOWLEDGE CAN ONLY BE GOOD. LEST THE TORCH WHICH IS NOW BURNING LOW GO OUT FOREVER, I PLACE A SPARK FROM IT HERE TO REKINDLE IT IN FUTURE AGES.

IN THIS VAULT, THERE ARE BOOKS WHICH EXPLAIN WHAT WE KNOW OF SCIENCE AND HISTORY, STARTING WITH SIMPLE THINGS WHICH ANYONE CAN UNDERSTAND AND GOING ON TO THE PROUDEST DISCOVERIES OF THE HUMAN RACE. OUR SMALLER TOOLS AND MACHINES ARE HERE, AND MODELS OF THE LARGER ONES, TO HELP YOU LEARN AND REBUILD. HERE, TOO, ARE WHAT I COULD GATHER OF THE GREAT PROPHETS AND PHILOSOPHERS AND ARTISTS FROM ALL OUR PAST AGES, TO EXPLAIN HOW A REGAINED POWER SHOULD BE USED WITH MORE WISDOM AND KINDNESS THAN OUR UNHAPPY WORLD HAS SHOWN, AND TO INSPIRE YOU NOT MERELY TO IMITATE US, BUT TO GO ON FOR YOURSELVES AND CREATE NEWER AND BETTER DREAMS OF YOUR OWN.

GUARD THIS TREASURE. USE IT WELL. MAY GOD HELP YOU IN YOUR TASK AND IN YOUR TRIUMPHS.

It was long before Carl had finished spelling it out, and he had not understood much of what was in the message. But he knew it was a cry across the ages, and tears stung his eyes.

"Who did this?" he whispered.

"I don't know," answered Ronwy as softly. "It must have been a scientist who foresaw the Doom, five hundred years ago, and tried to save this for us. But his name is nowhere here. I think," he added after a moment, "that he didn't want us to know his name, that he wanted us to think of the whole human race, which had created all this, as giving it to us."

"And the vault is tabooed!" Carl's bitter cry sent the echoes booming hollowly from wall to wall.

"It need not always be so," replied Ronwy. "Someday, when you are Chief of the Dalesmen, you may be able to get the taboo lifted. It will take the work of many men and many years to learn all that is in here and put it to use. In a lifetime of study, I have only mastered a tiny part of this great store. Come." He took Carl's hand. "Let me show you a little."

It was a strange quest, hunting among these dusty cases and boxes, lifting books and plans and models in trembling hands, there in the vault where time—yes, time itself—had been caged. Carl's mind staggered from most of the writings and machines. But there were things which could be used right now, today! A new design of sailboat, a windmill, a ritual called *vaccination* for preventing the dreaded smallpox, the natural laws of heredity by which farmers could breed better grain and livestock—a whole new world lay under his hands!

Tom picked up one thing, a short metal tube with glass in one end and a crank on the side. "What is this?" he asked.

Ronwy smiled in the yellow candle glow. "Turn the crank," he said.

Tom did, and yelled in astonishment as a clear, white beam of light sprang from the glass. He dropped the thing—Carl snatched it out of the air—and the light died away.

"It's called a flashlight," said Ronwy. "It has to be hand-powered, the card by it said, because the *batteries* they once had wouldn't last many years."

Carl turned the miracle over in his fingers. "May I keep this?" he asked. "I'll need something to prove what I say when I bring this story back to Dalestown."

It was Ronwy's turn to be surprised. "What do you mean?" he asked.

Carl's eyes gleamed fierce. "I mean that tomorrow night we

three will try to sneak past those Lann scouts and get home,'' he answered. ''Then the Dalesmen will come here in force, take over the vault, learn how to make weapons like the ancients had—and drive the invaders away!''

There was a silence, then—

''*If* we get past the Lann,'' said Owl.

CHAPTER 4

The Undying Light

ANOTHER day went by, a day of restlessly prowling the ruins under the hostile eyes of the witch-folk, and slowly the sun crossed heaven and limned the high, stern towers black against a ruddy western sky. Carl, Tom, and Owl fetched their horses, which had been stabled in an old place of polished marble known as BANK, and began readying themselves for their journey.

"The Lann may have gone away," said Owl hopefully.

"I'm afraid not," answered Carl. "They're scared of the City, but at the same time they know it's well for them to stop any messages going between the witches and the Dalesmen. They'll have at least a few men waiting outside to catch us." He smiled, trying to ignore the coldness of his hands and the tightness in his throat. "But it's a big woods and a dark night, so with fair luck we can slip by them. And if not—" He slapped his saddlebag. "If not, we may still have a chance."

"I am guilty," said Ronwy. "I am guilty of sending you out to your enemies, when you are my guests."

"You couldn't help it, sir," replied Tom quietly. "We know you're our friend."

"In the old days," said Ronwy, "you could have traveled from one end of America to another without fear. Now those few miles you have to go are one long deathtrap. If you get home, Carl—if you become Chief of the Dalesmen—remember that!"

"I will remember," said Carl.

He tied his pony's mouth shut so that it could not whinny and betray him; his comrades did the same. Clear and lovely overhead, the first stars winked through a gathering dusk.

"Good-by, Ronwy," said Carl. "And thank you."

"The gods go with you," said the old man.

He stood looking after them until their forms were lost in bush and shadow.

The boys walked, leading their horses. Night thickened until they were groping through a pit of darkness whose walls bulked ragged against the stars. Slowly, stumblingly, they made their way through tumbled wreckage and crackling brush until they stood at the edge of the City and looked out over a dim sweep of forest and meadow. Straining their ears, they could hear only the dry chirp of crickets and rustle of wind—once an owl hooted, once a wildcat screamed—but no sign of the enemy, no trace. Their own breathing seemed loud in the stillness, and Carl thought that surely the Lann must hear the drumbeats of his heart.

"We don't follow the highway out, do we?" whispered Tom.

"No, you woodenhead—that'd be a giveaway," answered Owl as quietly. "We strike out across country, eh, Carl?"

"Yes," nodded the Chief's son. "I think we can ride now, slowly, following the open land but keeping in the shadow of trees." He hooked one foot in the stirrup and swung into his saddle. "Let's go."

His tautened ears heard the night murmurous around him. The long grass whispered under hoofs, leaves brushed his cheek as he hugged the line of forest, a stone clinked and his muscles knotted with alarm. Slowly—softly—the City was lost behind him, trees closed in, he was back in the wilderness.

The Lann weren't stupid, he thought. They'd have known their prey would try slipping past them. So unless they had ringed in the whole City—which was hardly possible—they would guard it with a few small bands of men scattered well apart and ranging the territory on a patrol which might or might not happen close enough for a hunter's keen ears to hear the faint noise of passage. It lay with the gods.

The meadow ended in a wall of forest. Carl urged his pony forward through a line of hedge that snapped and rustled and brought the sweat out cold on his forehead. Beyond, there was gloom in which the high trunks were like pillars holding up a roof of night. The horses stumbled on rough ground, and Carl hoped he could find his directions. It would be a terrible joke if they spent all night circling back to the City.

"*Listen!*"

Tom's hissing word brought Carl erect in the saddle, reining in his mount and staring wildly through darkness. Yes—yes—the sound of hoofs, the rattle of iron. . . . He held back a groan. The Lann!

"Wait a bit," Carl breathed. "They may pass by."

The noise grew louder, nearer, and he realized that the patrol would likely pass close enough to hear the horses' stamping and heavy breathing. Now there was nothing for it but to run.

Leaning over, the pony's mane rough against his bare arm, he eased off the gagging rope. The animal would need its mouth for gulping air, he thought grimly, and almost smiled when it whickered its relief. "This way," he said. "Back—out to the meadows—"

"Hey-ah! Who goes there?"

The deep-throated shout rang between the trees. Carl urged his pony to a trot, though branches were whipping his face, and heard the voices of the Lann rise in excitement behind him. Now the hunt began!

Breaking out into the open again, he struck heels against his pony's ribs and felt the rhythm of gallop under him. Tom and Owl edged their bigger horses alongside his, and for a brief while only the thudding of hoofs broke the night.

Behind, a blot of darkness came out of the woods and became half a dozen riders. Starlight gleamed on helmets and lances, and a horn blew its call as the Lann saw the boys ahead of them. Carl bent low in the saddle and went flying up a long slope of hillside.

Up and over! The swale below was thick with night. Rocks clattered and rang under frantic hoofs, and trees leaped out of nowhere to claw at eyes. The Lann topped the ridge and loomed against the sky, yelling.

Owl's horse stumbled on a root and went rolling. Catlike, the rider was out of the stirrups and falling clear. "Go on!" he yelled, rising to his knees. "Go on—get away!"

"No!" Tom reined in, brought his horse dancing back, and starlight was dim on his drawn sword. "No—we'll fight!"

Carl reined his own steed to a plunging halt and turned around. Now it was too late. The Lann were racing down the slope, howling their glee, no chance to escape them.

Unless—

Bending over, Carl groped in his saddlebag. The metal of the thing he sought was cold in his hand as he lifted it free.

The Lann slowed and approached at a walk. Carl saw the flash of eyes and teeth in bearded faces, spiked iron helmets and polished leather breastplates shimmered faintly, lances were brought to rest. The leader raised his voice: "Do you surrender?"

"No!" yelled Carl. The echoes went ringing and bouncing between the stony heights, no, no, no.

"We come from the City," Carl shouted as loudly and wrathfully as his lungs could endure. "We come with the black magic of the Doom that wastes the world, the glowing death, nine thousand devils chained and raging to be free. Depart, men of Lann, for we are witches!"

The horsemen waited. Carl heard a breath sucked between teeth in the quiet of night, saw a shield lifted and a charm fingered. But they did not run.

"I hold the glowing death!" screamed Carl. "Your flesh will rot from your bones, your eyes will fall from the sockets, you are dead men already! See, men of Lann, see!"

He aimed the flashlight and whirled the crank. A white beam stabbed forth, picking a savage face out of a night which suddenly seemed blacker, swinging around to another and another. A horse neighed, and a man shouted.

Carl let go the handle, and it whined eerily to silence as the light died. Then he cranked again, holding the beam like a pointed spear, and urged his horse forward. As he advanced, he threw back his head and howled like a wild dog.

A single noise of terror broke from the warriors, splitting the patrol into a crazed scramble of hoofs and bodies scattered in all directions. In moments, the men were lost to sight and sound.

Carl sat for a minute, not daring to believe, and then he began to laugh.

By dawn, the boys had come most of the way. Carl's flashlight trick would hardly work in the daytime, so as the first dull gray of morning stole into the sky, they dismounted, rubbed down their weary horses, and rolled up in blankets to sleep for a while. But the sun was not far over the horizon before they were on the trail again.

"We'll be back just about in time for the chores," grumbled Owl, but the eyes twinkled in his round face.

Tom ran a hand through his fiery hair. "It seems as if we left an age ago," he said, with a puzzled note in his voice. "We've seen and done and learned so much—I hardly know what to believe any longer." He glanced at Carl. "Tell me, is everything false that they taught us? Are there really no devils or magic or Doom?"

"I don't know," said Carl soberly. "I suppose the old stories are true enough as far as they go—only they don't go far enough, and it's up to us to find the whole truth. The Doctors, who claim to have kept as much of the old wisdom as is good for men to know, don't want us to do that; but I think that between the need of the Dalesmen for help against the Lann and this proof in my saddlebag, we can convince the people otherwise." He yawned and stretched his stiffened muscles. "It'll be good to reach your father's place. I could use a hot breakfast!"

They followed the woodland trail through the cool rustling green, and John's sons spied the landmarks with eager eyes. It was Tom who first sniffed the air and turned back a worried face. "Do you smell smoke?" he asked.

In a short while Carl and Owl sensed it too, the thin bitter reek and a light bluish haze in the air. They clucked to their horses and broke into a weary trot, straining homeward.

Out of the woods, over a rise of ground, and then the dear, broad fields of home—

The farm was burnt.

They sat for a long time, stunned, only slowly grasping the ruin which was here. The outbuildings were smoking heaps from which charred rafters stuck up like fingers pointing at an empty heaven. The house was still burning here and there. Little flames wavered over fallen beams and blowing ash. Smoke stained the cloudless sky, black and ugly, and there was a terrible silence everywhere.

"Father." It was a whimper in Owl's throat. "Mother."

"Come *on!*" Tom took the lead, whipping his horse ruthlessly to a gallop. The others followed, sobbing without shame.

Carl, less grief stricken than the brothers, rode about the yard scanning it for signs. The ground was trampled by many hoofs, the pens were broken open and a trail went through the grain fields toward the east. "The Lann," he said thinly. "A party of Lann warriors came and burned the place and drove off the stock to feed their army."

Tom and Owl, white-faced, were poking through the smoldering, flickering wreck of the house. They looked up as Carl approached. "No bodies," said Tom. "We haven't found any dead."

"No—" Carl went over to the shed. It had not burned so thoroughly as the rest, and he could see tools lying in the blackened wood. But no sign of the wagon which every farm owned. . . .

"Be glad," he said, forcing a smile. "See, the wagon's gone, and there are no dead here. That meant your people fled before the enemy came. They should be on their way to Dalestown now."

Owl let out a whoop, and Tom managed to laugh. It could have been worse. They dared not think how much worse.

"Unless the Lann took them captive," Tom worried.

"No. Why should invaders bother with prisoners?" Carl looked anxiously about the horizon. An evil black smudge to the west showed that another place had also been sacked. "But the Lann did this only lately, last night I suppose. That means they're still hereabouts. We'd better get moving!"

There was little cover in the cleared farm lands. The boys went slowly down a rutted, dusty road, scanning the land nervously for signs of the enemy. Now and again they passed another gutted place where bodies sprawled in the fields and masterless animals ran loose—but nowhere a living human, in all the wasted marches.

They had eaten their last supplies, and hunger gnawed at them. Carl's bow brought down a strayed pig, but he would only let them cut a few pieces of meat from it to eat uncooked. A fire could draw enemy attention. They chewed on raw pork and plodded gloomily forward.

Their direction was southwest, toward the great forest which bordered the Dalesmen's territory. That would be safer to travel through until the last dash across open country to Dalestown, and Carl reasoned that the fleeing border dwellers would have taken the same route. In midafternoon, the boys were glad of their decision. They saw a column of dust far down the road and hastened to a clump of trees. Hiding in the thicket, they saw a troop of Lann warriors riding past.

The stocky men sat their shaggy mounts as if they were part of the animals. Helmets blinked in the sunlight. The polished leather of shields and breastplates gleamed over jagged, fierce-colored paint. Long roweled spurs hung at the heels of fur-trimmed boots. Lances rose and fell in the rhythm of motion. Cloaks and red banners flapped against the green and brown of earth. The harsh, tanned faces were dark with beard and braided hair, eyes roved restlessly, and teeth flashed white at some jest. Spread over the plain, businesslike, warrior harness was barbaric finery—not only the men's own earrings and bracelets—but plunder from Dale homes, necklaces draped around hairy throats, jeweled rings flashing on sinewy fingers, silken cloth blowing from shoulders and waists.

They rode past, and the noise of them—clash and jingle of iron, squeaking of leather, thud of hoofs, hard, barking laughter—faded into the hot summer stillness. Carl, Tom, and Owl looked at each other with dismay. They saw too plainly that the Lann *had* struck through this part of the border; that the gathered farmers, if they had even had time to assemble, had been routed by their attack; and that a host was readying itself to fall on Dalestown. Time was shorter than even Chief Ralph had thought—desperately, terribly short. The vision of defeat and slavery was ghastly before Carl's eyes.

CHAPTER 5

Return—and Retreat

THE SUN was lowering again when the boys came to the western edge of the farm lands and entered the woods. Their horses slogged along in headdrooping weariness and they themselves felt aching bones and sandy eyelids. But need drove them, a need of a hiding place from the ranging Lann and a need, still greater and more bitter, to know what had happened to their people.

Carl threw one last glance behind him. The Dales rolled green and still and beautiful away to the east, and the quiet evening air was full of sunset and the sleepy twitter of birds. No other human was in sight. Oh, it was a broad and fair land, and he knew what sort of hunger was in the Lann for such a home. But by all the gods, he thought with an anger dulled by his tiredness, it was the Dalesmen's home first!

The road had narrowed to a single track, and once under the trees it became a grassy lane where the hoofs were muffled and rabbits fled startled before the riders. They passed a charcoal burner's lonely hut, abandoned now in the face of the Lann. "That's the last dwelling," said Tom, his voice flat and empty. "After this, there's only the wilderness."

A little way beyond, the trail petered out altogether and there was nothing. But here another pathway ran into the first, and Carl bent low over it, straining his eyes in the twilight.

"Look!" he cried. "Look here—spoor of travelers!"

They saw it then: fresh wheel tracks and hoofprints, broken twigs, and a trampled way plunging into the forest. Owl let out a faint yip. "It may be our own folks!" he chattered. "They could've come by the road past Harry's instead of the one we took—it'd lead them here—Come on, fellows! Come *on!*"

The dusk rose between the high trunks like mist, and, winding around the trees, it was hard to follow even the plain wagon trail over the hilly ground. Carl's pony gasped under him, and he patted the bowed neck. "Easy, old man, easy," he whispered. "It can't be far now. A loaded wagon can't travel fast through this stuff."

"Look! Up ahead!" Tom pointed a shadowy arm through the deepening twilight. A ruddy spark danced waveringly beyond a tinkle of stream. "A campfire!"

Too tired to think whether those might be Lann who had made it, the boys forded the brook and scrambled with their mounts up the farther bank. Yes, yes . . . a small fire, picking out the shapes of two wagons and tethered animals . . . a man leaning on his spear. . . .

"Who's that?" The voice rolled forth, weary and shaken. "Halt or we shoot!"

"Father!" yelled Owl joyfully. He sprang from his horse and ran toward the sentry. Tom plunged after him, and Carl was not far behind. When the Chief's son arrived, John the farmer was embracing his boys and crying praises to all the gods, while their mother wept her joy. In the ruins of their world, they still had each other!

The dim red flicker of light picked out other faces, an old man, his son with wife and baby, and a young woman. They must have joined forces as they escaped. There were four brawny oxen to pull the wagons, a string of horses, and a couple of dogs, all resting under the trees. The wagons were piled high with family goods, and Carl frowned even as his hand was being shaken. What was the use of dragging all that through heartbreaking miles of forest when it slowed travel and invited raiders?

Well. . . . He remembered what his father had once said: "People are people, you can't change them much and a Chief has to take them as they are. Never forget that it's their will which keeps him Chief."

He wondered with a sick fear what had happened to his father in these last long days. Were the Lann already at Dalestown?

Carl eased himself to the cool, damp earth, looked into the sputtering flames, and listened drowsily to John's account of what had come to pass. Even if the story was grim, it was good to sprawl again and rest.

Scouts had brought word the very day the boys had left John's homestead, that the Lann vanguard was emerging from the woods near by and gathering itself in the fields. The war-word had gone on hurried feet from house to lonely house, but it had taken more than a day to assemble the men, and they met the enemy weary from a night's hard traveling.

"They scattered us," said John somberly. "Their horsemen outflanked our pikemen and struck us from the side and behind. We fought long and hard. Many died in their tracks, but the others broke us up into little knots of men and finally we ran. The Lann hunted us down. They hunted us like dogs harrying a rabbit. Only nightfall saved us, and we streamed home knowing we were beaten. The Lann ranged about, plundering wherever they came, but that may have been a good thing. It held them up long enough for us to flee."

If the northern farmers had gone to Dalestown in the first place, joined themselves to a large army under a leader who knew something of warcraft . . . Carl clamped his mouth shut on the words that he knew were too late.

"There are many families retreating like us through the woods," said the young man, Torol. "It's slow going, but I don't think the Lann will bother chasing us. They've richer booty at hand—our homes." He spat. His wife started to cry, softly and hopelessly, and he put an arm about her shoulder and murmured what empty comfort he could.

Carl reflected that the business of sacking the northern marches would keep the invaders occupied for a while. Then they would also have to assemble their entire army—a part of which had fought here. And, while they seemed to have a cavalry such as none of the southern tribes had ever dreamed of, the bulk of their host must be footmen just as it was in the Dales. So all in all, he thought Ralph would have a few days' grace yet before the hammer blow fell.

Nevertheless, he wanted to get home and join his father as soon as possible. He groaned at the thought of creaking through brush and hills with these overloaded oxcarts, and thought for a moment of leaving the group and pushing on alone. But no—his eyes went to the tired, dusty faces of Tom and Owl—those two had followed him, stood by him like true comrades in the face of the unknown powers of the City. Now they were with their folk, and the little caravan would need every hunter it could get to keep itself fed on the way. "The Chief," Ralph had said, "is the first servant of the tribe."

Carl shook his head, sighing, and spread a blanket roll for sleep. He would let John's sons tell about the expedition to the witch-folk. Just now, he wanted only to rest.

The following day grew into a slow nightmare of travel. For all the straining and grunting of oxen, and even the horses hitched on in especially difficult places, the wagons made no speed. They were snared in brush and saplings, stuck in the muddy banks of streams, dangerously tipped in the wild swoop of hillsides and gullies. Men had to push from behind, chop a path in front, guide the stubborn beasts along rugged slopes, cursing and sweating and always listening for the war whoop of the Lann. Near evening, Carl shuddered with relief when John asked him to go hunting.

The boy took bow and arrows, a light spear, and a rawhide lariat, and slipped quietly into the tangled woods. His aching shoulders straightened as he moved away from the creaking wagons, and he sniffed the rich green life about him with a new delight. Summer, leaves rustling and breaking the light into golden flecks, a glimpse of blue sky amid cool shadows, a king snake sunning itself on a moss-grown log, a pheasant rising on alarmed wings before he could shoot, like a rainbowed lightning flash—oh, it was good to be alive, alive and free in the young summer! Carl whistled to himself until he was out of earshot of the caravan, then he grew still and his flitting brown form mingled with the shade. He had some work to do.

It didn't take long to spot a woodchuck's burrow—but was the animal at home? Carl fitted an arrow to his bowstring and lay down to wait. The sun crept westward, his nose itched, flies buzzed maddeningly around his sweat-streaked face, but he crouched like a cat until patience was rewarded. The woodchuck crept from its hole, Carl's bow twanged, and he slung his prey at his belt. Nice fat one. But it would take more than that to feed ten people. Carl went on his way.

He shot at a squirrel and missed, not feeling too sorry about it, for he liked the impudent red dwarfs. Scrambling along a slope, he met a porcupine and added it to his bag. The hill went down to a thin, trickling brook which he followed, picking up a small turtle on the way. Mixed food tonight. But not very much yet, even if Tom and Owl were ranging elsewhere. . . .

Hold—what was that, up ahead?

Carl splashed along the brook until it ran off a stony bluff into a broad, quiet pool under the mournful guarding of a willow thicket. The ground about the water hole was muddy with trampling. This was where some worth-while game drank! Carl didn't care to wait alone for it after dark. He knew the large difference between courage and foolishness. Next evening he and someone else could return. The caravan wouldn't be many miles away then, he thought impatiently.

No—wait! Something else—

Carl chuckled to himself as he saw the broad, hard-packed trail running from the pool. A cowpath, but it was the rangy, dangerous herds of woods-running wild cattle which had beaten that road through the forest. He knew that such trails often ran nearly straight for a score of miles. If this one did, the wagons could follow it, the trek home would become easy and swift, and . . .

Skirting the pool, he ran down the trail at a long lope to check. What if he didn't bring back any more game? This news was worth a hungry night. He'd follow the path a mile or two to make sure. The trees flowed past, and evening quiet dropped over the land, muffling all but the calling of birds and the soft thud of his own moccasined feet, running and running.

When he stopped, wiping the sweat from his face and laughing aloud in glee—yes, the trail could easily be used—he grew aware that the shadows were very long. In his excitement he'd gone farther than was wise and now he couldn't make it back before nightfall.

"Stupid," he muttered. But there had, after all, not been much choice, and in any case he had little to fear. He started back, walking this time. The sunset air was cool on his face and under his wet shirt. He shivered and hastened his steps.

Night deepened as the sun went under the hills. Shadows ebbed and flowed around him, creeping from the brake, flooding softly between the trees. A single pure star blinked forth, white in the dusk-blue sky over the trail. An owl hooted and a wildcat squalled answer, far off in the woods. Somewhere a deer ran off in terror. It could be near or far, the leaves played strange tricks with sound, and now the very light was becoming as queer and magical. Carl thought of the godling spirits which were said to haunt the lonely glens. A thin white streamer of mist curled before him, and in spite of his City-strengthened doubts, he muttered a guardian charm.

Willows hung dark against a glooming heaven, the pool was up ahead and fog was smoking out of it to blur the last remnants of sight. Carl picked a slow way through the weeping branches, skirting the white, mysterious glimmer of mist and water.

Something moved in the twilight. Carl stiffened and an icy flash stabbed along his spine. The thing ahead was a deeper blot of darkness, rippling and flowing as if it were a mist-wraith too, but it was big, it was huge, and the last wan light threw back a cold green look of eyes.

Carl backed up, hefting his spear, until he stood in the cow trail again. The beast edged out of the thicket and crouched. Its tail lashed and a growl rumbled in its throat.

A tiger!

There were not many of the huge striped cats this far north, but they were cursed and dreaded as killers of sheep and cattle and sometimes men. To the tribes, there had always been tigers—they had no way of knowing that these were the descendants of animals escaped from zoos in the Doom. This one must have been lying in wait for the herds to come to drink, and was angered by Carl's disturbance, angry enough, perhaps, to look on him as a meal.

Slowly, hardly daring to move, Carl leaned his spear against the tree at his back. It wouldn't do much good if the beast charged. He drew out a fistful of arrows, slipped the bow off his shoulder, and strung it with one gasping motion. It was a better weapon.

The tiger snarled, flattening its belly to the ground. The smell of blood from the bag of game at Carl's waist must have stirred its hunter's heart. The boy fitted an arrow to the string and drew the bow taut. His pulse roared in his ears.

The tiger crept nearer.

The bow sang, and the tiger screamed and launched itself. Carl sprang aside almost as he shot. The tiger hit the ground where he had been and threshed about, biting at the arrow in its shoulder. Carl picked another arrow off the ground where he had thrown them, drew the bow and let loose. He couldn't see in the murk if he had hit or not. The tiger staggered to its feet, growling. Before the tawny thunderbolt could strike again, Carl's bow had hummed afresh.

The tiger screamed again and turned away. Yelling, Carl groped for another arrow. He fired and missed, but the beast was loping in a three-legged retreat. As Carl sank shaking to the ground, he felt blood hot and wet beneath him.

If the tiger lived, he thought without exultation—he was still too frightened himself for that—it would have a proper respect for mankind.

The thought continued as he resumed his way. It wasn't the animals which man had to fear. Tiger, bear, snake, even the terrible dog packs could not face human fire and metal. Slowly, as men hewed down the wilderness, its snarling guardians were driven back. Their fight was hopeless.

And in the City, it had began to dawn on him that not even the supernatural, demons and ghosts and the very gods, threatened men. The powers of night and storm, flood and fire and drought and winter, were still a looming terror, but they had been conquered once by the ancients and they could be harnessed again.

No, man's remorseless and deadly foe was only—himself.

But *that* enemy was old and strong and crafty. It had brought to agonized wreck the godlike civilization of the ancients. Today, in the form of taboo and invading barbarians, it was risen afresh, and seemed all too likely to win.

Overwhelming despair replaced Carl's fear. Could the children of light ever win? he thought. Must the Dalesmen go down in flame and death before the trampling horses of Lann? Must the last gasp of ancient wisdom rust away in darkness? Could there ever be a victory?

CHAPTER 6

Taboo!

FOLLOWING the wild cattle trail, John's party took only another day and a half to get through the western forest to the point where he had meant to strike east for Dalestown. The wagons lay in the cover of brush at the edge of cultivation, while Tom and Carl rode out to find if the settled lands were still free.

The boys returned jubilantly by sundown. "There's been no fighting around here," said Carl. "As far as the people we talked to know, the Lann haven't gotten farther yet than the northern border."

"That's far enough," said John bleakly. Strain and sorrow had made him gaunt in the last few days. His eyes were hollow and he seldom smiled. But he nodded his unkempt head now. They'd have a safe passage to Dalestown; that was something.

At dawn the caravan stirred, and wagons creaked through long, dew-wet grass until they emerged in open country and found one of the pitted dirt roads of the tribe. There Carl took his leave of them. "You don't need me any longer," he said. "There are no enemies here, and the farmers will give you food and shelter. But it will take you perhaps two days to reach the town, and I have news for my father which can scarcely wait."

"Aye, go then—and thank you, Carl," said John.

"Father, how about letting me go along?" asked Owl. "It's just driving from here on, no work—and it's awful slow!"

A tired, lopsided smile crossed the man's bearded face. "All right, Jim," he agreed. "And I daresay Tom would like to follow. I'll meet you in town, boys."

The red-haired lad flashed a grin. "Thanks," he said. "I just want to see people's faces when Carl shows them that magic light."

The three friends saddled their horses and trotted swiftly down the road. Before long, the wagons were lost to sight and they rode alone.

The country was fair with hills, and valleys green with ripening crops, tall, windy groves of trees, the metal blink of streams and lakes, and shadows sweeping over the sunlit breadth of land. The farms were many, and wooden fences held the sleek livestock grazing in pastures. Most of the homes were the usual log cabins, larger or smaller depending on the wealth of the man and the size of his family, but some of the richer estates had two-story houses of stone and square-cut timbers. Now and again the travelers passed through a hamlet of four or five buildings—a smithy, a trading post, a water-powered mill, a Doctor's house—but otherwise the Dales lay open. Smoke rose blue and wing-ragged from chimneys, and farmers hailed the boys as they went past.

Carl noticed that workers in the yards and the fields were almost entirely women, children, and old men. Those of fighting age were marshaled at Dalestown. And even these peaceful stay-at-homes carried spears and axes wherever they went. The shadow of war lay dark over the people.

On rested horses, the ride to town took only a day. In the late afternoon, Carl topped a high ridge and saw his goal in the valley below him.

Not much more than a village as the ancients had reckoned such things, it was still the only real town that the tribe had. Here the folk came to barter and make merry; here the Chief and the High Doctor lived, and the tribesmen met to vote on laws and action; here the four great seasonal feasts were held each year; and here the warriors assembled in time of danger. That was the first thing Carl noticed as his eyes swept the scene: tents and wooden booths clustered about the town to house the men, wagons drawn up and horses grazing in the fields, smoke of cooking fires staining the sky. As he rode down the hill, he caught the harsh reflection of sunlight on naked iron.

A twenty-foot stockade rising out of high banks inclosed Dalestown in four walls. At each corner stood a wooden watchtower, with catapults and stone-throwing engines mounted just under the roof. In each wall, gates of heavy timber, reinforced with metal, protected the entrances. The town had fought off enemy attacks before. Carl hoped it would not have to do so again.

He and his friends picked a threading way between the camps of the warriors. It was a brawling, lusty sight, with beardless youths and scarred old veterans swarming over the trampled grass. Sitting before their tents, they sharpened weapons and polished armor. Some were gathered about a fire and sang to the strum of a banjo while the evening meal bubbled in a great kettle. Others wrestled, laughed and bragged of what they would do, but Carl saw many who sat quiet and moody, thinking of the defeat in the north and wondering how strong the wild horsemen of Lann were.

The main gate, on the south side, stood open, and a restless traffic swirled back and forth between the armed guards. One of them hailed the Chief's son: "Hi, there, Carl! So you're back? I thought the devils in the City would have eaten you."

"Not yet, Ezzef." Carl smiled at the young pikeman, gay in red cloak and polished iron cuirass. Ezzef was one of the Chief's regular guardsmen, who ordinarily existed to keep order in the town. Carl and he had long been friends.

"No, you're too ornery to make a decent meal." More soberly, Ezzef came over to stand at Carl's stirrup and look up into his dusty, sun-darkened face. "Did you make the bargain, Carl? Will the witch-men forge for us?"

"The Chief has to know first. It's a long story," said the boy, turning his eyes away. He didn't want to start panic among the men by rumors of the City people's refusal, or premature hopes by tales of magic powers.

Ezzef nodded gravely and went back to his post, and Carl began to realize the loneliness of a leader. He couldn't share his journey with this old comrade—the tribe had to come before any one man— but it was hard. He clicked his tongue, and the pony moved forward again, shoving slowly through the crowds.

Within the stockade, Dalestown was a jumble of wooden houses through which muddy streets wound a narrow way. It had its own wells and cisterns, and Ralph had, several years before, caused others to be made so that fire fighters would always have water close at hand. One bit of ancient wisdom which the Doctors told the people was that filth meant plague, so there were public baths and the Chief paid men to haul away wastes. But with all those who had crowded in since the first threat of war, that system was in danger of breakdown.

As Carl rode down High Street, between the tall, overhanging walls of buildings gaudily painted under splashes of mud, he saw the same confusion of people he had known and loved all his life. Here, a rich merchant passed by, dressed in furs and gold chains, borne in a litter by four half-naked servants. There, a group of children tumbled and rolled in the dust; a mongrel yapped at their play. Yonder came a housewife, her long skirts lifted above the littered street, a baby strapped into a carrying-cradle on her back. A wandering juggler, his lean body clad in fantastically colored rags, a banjo slung next to his ribs, brushed shoulders with a sober-faced young Doctor in the long blue robe of his order, carrying a bag of magical instruments. Circled by the perpetual bustle, a tall, black-skinned trader in clothes of foreign cut, come from the southern tribes to barter his cotton or fruit or tobacco for the furs and leather of the Dales, was talking to a white-bearded old farmer who stood unmoving in his wooden shoes, puffing a long-stemmed pipe. A bulky guard was warning two drunken warriors to behave themselves; a wagonload of fine timber moved slowly toward some carpenter's shop; and a horse tamer edged his half-broken mount carefully through the swarm.

Open doors, and shingled booths, where the work of the town went on, lined the sides of the street. A smith, muscled and sooty, hammered out a plowshare in the ruddy glow of his fire. Across the way, a fat baker gave two round loaves of coarse black bread, new and warm and fragrant, to a boy. And a weaver had his cloths and rugs spread out for sale, next door to a tailor who sat cross-legged making complete garments. On the corner, a dark and smoky tavern rang with noisy life and beside the tavern, a trader's store was massed with foreign goods and delicate jewelry for sale. Even now, Dalestown tried to live as it had always done.

But many newcomers filled the streets, leaning from the windows and jamming into the crowd. Refugees, thought Carl, men and women and children from outlying farms who had fled here for safety when news of the invaders came. Some could stay with friends and relatives, some could pay for a bed in one of the few inns—but most had to sleep outside, in tents or under their wagons, ready to flee inside the walls if danger threatened. Their eyes were filled with fear and a deep, hopeless longing, their voices shrill or else hushed to an unnatural quiet. It was not a good thing to see, and Carl touched the saddlebag where he had the magic light as if groping for comfort.

The boys came out on the open market square in the center of town and forced a slow path across its packed width. The Hall loomed on the farther side, a great building of dark oak with painted gables and the heads of animals carved along the eaves and ridgepole. Here was the place of meeting for the tribe. On its right was the smaller house of the Chief, squarely and solidly built of wood and stone, the banner of the Dales—a green fir tree on a background of gold—floating above it. Toward this Carl directed his horse.

An old servant stood on the porch, looking unhappily over the restless throng. When he saw Carl, he shouted. "Master Carl! Oh, Master Carl, you're back! Thank the gods, you're back!"

"You never doubted it, did you, Rob?" smiled Carl, touched at the welcome. He swung stiffly to the ground, and the old man patted his shoulder with a thin, blue-veined hand.

"Oh, but it's been so long, Master Carl—"

"Only a few days. Is my father inside?"

"Yes, he's talking with the High Doctor. Go right in, Master Carl, go in and make him glad. I'll take your horse."

"And my friends' horses too, please." Carl frowned. He wasn't overly happy at having to confront Donn before he had talked with his father. The High Doctor meant well, and was kindly enough when no one crossed him, but he was overbearing and tightly bound by the ancient laws.

Well, it would have to be faced sometime. "Come on, boys," said Carl, mounting the steps.

"Maybe we should wait," hedged Tom.

"Nonsense. You're the guests of the house, as your folks'll be when they arrive. Follow me."

Carl entered a hallway paneled in wood and carpeted with skins. Light from the windows was getting dim, and candles burned in their brackets on the wall. It was a large, well-furnished house, but there were grander places in town. The Chief's power did not lie in trade goods.

A small thunderbolt came shouting down the stairs and threw itself into Carl's arms, squealing and shouting. "Hello, brat," said the boy gruffly. "Get down—the Lann don't do as much damage as you."

It was his young sister Betty, five years old, who clung to him and stared with wide eyes. There were only these two left—Ralph's other children, and then his wife, had died, of some disease which the ancients could have cured but which was too strong for the drums and prayers and herbs of the Doctors, and the Chief had not married again. The three were a happy family, but there were dark memories among them.

"What's 'at?" Betty pointed to the flashlight, wrapped in a piece from his tattered cloak, that Carl bore in one hand.

"Magic, brat, magic. Now where's Daddy?"

"In'a living room. Can I come?"

"Well—" Carl hesitated. It might not be wise for a child to know of this and prattle the news all over town. If the Lann were as smart as he thought, they had a few spies mingled with the refugees. "Not just now. This is man-talk. Later, huh?"

Betty made fewer objections than he had thought—she was growing up enough to learn that men ruled the tribes, under the law if not always in fact—and he sent her trotting back up the stairs. Then he led Tom and Owl down the hall to the living-room door. He opened it softly and looked in.

The room was long and low, furnished with a dark richness of carved wood and thick skins and the trophies of war and hunt. Light from many candles and the broad stone fireplace filled the farther end with radiance and shadows, glimmering off shields and swords hung above the mantel, off wrought brass candlesticks and silver plates. Windows between heavy draperies showed the last gleam of day.

Ralph stood before the hearth. He was a tall and powerful man of thirty-seven, his eyes blue in a grave bronzed face, his hair and close-cropped beard the color of gold. His dress was, as usual, simple: plain shirt and breeches of linen, a green wool cloak swinging from broad shoulders, a dagger at his tooled leather belt. His big hands were calloused with labor, for he worked his own farm outside the walls, but his look was calm and strong, and Carl's heart quickened at the sight of him.

Old Donn sat in a chair by the hearth, blue robe drawn tight around his gaunt frame. Like the other Doctors, he was clean-shaven, and only a thin, white halo of hair fringed his high skull.

With his hooked nose and sunken cheeks and smoldering, steady eyes, he resembled an aged eagle. One bony hand rested on the serpent-wreathed wand of his authority where it was laid across his knees; he rested his chin in his other, as he looked across at the third man.

This was a stranger, a lean young warrior of about twenty, weaponless and clad in garments obviously borrowed from Ralph. His hair was raven black, and a dark mustache crossed his sharp face. He was seated at ease, legs crossed, a hard and hostile smile on his mouth.

"It makes no difference," he was saying. "Whether you hold me or not, Raymon will come. He has other sons—"

"Carl!" Ralph saw the boy and took a long stride forward across the tiger-skin, his arms opening and sudden gladness lighting in his face. "Carl—you're back!"

They shook hands, father and son, and Ralph checked himself, putting on the mask of coolness expected from a man. Perhaps only Carl saw the candlelight glisten off a tear. It must have been cruel to hear that the enemy had been in the very region where he had sent his only son, the only hope of his race.

"Yes—Father." The boy cleared his throat, trying to get the thickness out of his voice. "Yes—I'm back, well and sound. And these are my friends, Tom and Owl—Jim, sons of John in the north—"

"Be welcome, friends of Carl and friends of mine," said Ralph gravely. He lifted his voice in a yell for a servant. "Margo, Margo, you human turtle, bring food and drink! Carl is back!"

Donn looked keenly at the boys. "And how did the trip to the City go?" he murmured.

"Both well and ill, sir," answered Carl uneasily. "But, Father— who is this?"

Ralph smiled with pride. "Carl, meet Lenard—eldest son of Raymon, Chief of the Lann!"

"What?" Tom's hand dropped unthinking to his knife.

"Aye, aye. There have been skirmishes in the north between our scouting parties and vanguard Lann troops." Ralph paced back to the hearth. "The other day our men brought back some prisoners taken in one of those fights, and among them was Lenard here. A valuable captive!"

Lenard grinned. "I was just explaining that my hostage value is small,'' he said in the harsh accents of the north. "We believe that the souls of dead warriors are reunited in Sky-Home, so—as long as my father has other brave sons—he will not betray our people to get me back.'' He waved a sinewy hand. ''But I must say my host Ralph has treated me well.''

''He gave oaths not to try to escape before battle is joined, and my guards wouldn't let him get out of the house in any event,'' said Ralph. ''I still think we can use him, . . . or at least learn from him.'' His eyes held a brief, desperate appeal. ''And if we treat our captives well, the Lann should do likewise—if they have honor.''

''We have honor,'' said Lenard stiffly, ''though it may not always be the same as yours.''

Carl folded his legs under him and sat down on the rug. He could not help a certain uneasiness at having Lenard so close. Lenard, the heir to the mastery over that savage horde which had chased him down the ways of night and laid the northern marches in ruin.

''But what of your journey, Carl?'' persisted Donn. ''What did the witch-folk say?''

Carl glanced at Lenard. The prisoner sat quietly leaning back, half in shadow, not even seeming to listen. And neither Ralph nor Donn seemed to care what he might learn.

Slowly, Carl told the story of his trip. There was stillness as he talked, under the thin dry crackle of flames. Once Donn stiffened and leaned forward, once Ralph whispered an oath and clenched his fists with a sudden blaze in his eyes—but both leaned away again, clamping the mask back over their faces, hooding eyes in the weaving shadow.

Night closed down outside, darkening the windows, stilling a little the babble of the aimless crowds. Wordlessly, the servant Margo came in with a tray of refreshment, set it on a table, and stole out again. Beyond the little ring of light at this end, the long room grew thick with a creeping darkness.

Under the light, Carl unwrapped the bundle in his hands. The ancient metal was smooth and cool; it seemed to vibrate with unknown powers. ''And this is the light,'' he said, his voice shaking ever so faintly. ''Look!''

He spun the crank, and the pure white beam sprang forth, searching out corners, flashing back from metal and darkly gleaming wood, a whisper of gears and a lance of cold, colorless fire. Ralph gasped, Lenard gripped the arms of his chair with sudden white-knuckled force—only Donn sat unmoving, unblinking, like the graven image of some eagle god.

It was to the Doctor that Carl first looked when he let the light die, for he knew that the real decision lay there. The class of the Doctors existed in all known tribes, men who handed down a fragment of the ancient wisdom and guarded the mysteries. A Doctor was many things: public scribe and record-keeper, teacher of the young, priest of the gods, medicine man in time of sickness, counselor and sorcerer and preserver of knowledge. Much of what they did was good—they knew some medicine and other things beneath all the magical rites, and their shrewd advice had helped many. But Carl thought that they were, in their hidebound beliefs and their fear of the Doom, the greatest reason why life had hardly changed in these hundreds of years. And the fountainhead of the Doctors was their grand master, Donn.

The old man was still very quiet. He had lifted his serpent wand, as if to ward off powers of evil, but his face did not move at all, he did not even seem to breathe.

"Carl—Carl—let me see that light!" Ralph stooped over his son, shaking with excitement, holding forth an eager hand. "Let me see it!"

"Stop."

Donn spoke softly. Little more than a whisper came from his thin lips, but it seemed to fill that room of tall shadows. He held out his own gaunt fingers. "Give it to me, Carl."

Slowly, as if moved by a power outside himself, Carl laid the metal tube in the hand of Donn.

"Taboo! Taboo!" The old pagan word rustled and murmured in dark corners, hooted mockingly up the chimney to hunt the wind. "It is forbidden."

"But it is *good!*" cried Carl, with a wrench in his soul. "It is the power which can save us from the Lann and—"

"It is one of the powers which brought the Doom." The High Doctor touched the flashlight with his wand and muttered some spell. "Would you unchain that wrath and fire again? Would you see the earth laid waste and the demons of Atmik raging over the sky and folk falling dead of fire and hunger and plague and the blue glow—cursing your name as they died? Taboo, taboo!"

Carl sat numbly, hardly aware of the stern words snapping from that suddenly grim face:

"You have broken the law. You entered the accursed City and consorted with witches. You opened a door on the powers of the Doom, and you brought one of those very devils home with you. Fools! You wanted to help the Dalesmen? Be glad you haven't destroyed them!"

After a moment, Donn spoke a little more gently. "Still, it is plain that some god protected you, for no harm that I can see has been done. I shall offer this light as a sacrifice to appease any anger in heaven. I shall throw it into the sacred well. And tomorrow you must come to the temple and have the sin taken off you—but that need only be marking your foreheads in the blood of a calf which you must bring. You meant well, and for that you shall be forgiven."

The sternness came back like the clash of iron chains: "But there shall be no more of this. Ralph, you know the law as well as I do, and we have both been lax about enforcing it. This is certainly not the first time a trader to the City went inside the taboo circle. But it shall be the last. From now on, the law of the Dales shall be carried out to the full. And that law says—for breaking the taboo on ancient works and magic, the penalty is death!"

CHAPTER 7

The Dalesmen Go to War

LOOKING into the wrathful eyes of Donn, Carl dared not argue further. He knew that this old man, who, in other times, had held him on his knee, given him toys and gifts, taught him the arts a Chief should know, would not hesitate to order him killed if he thought it was demanded by the gods. Tom and Owl shrank into the half-darkness beyond the firelight, afraid even to whisper. Ralph himself dropped his gaze and muttered surrender.

Donn's power was great in a very practical sense: he was the absolute ruler of the order of Doctors, which owned great lands and wealth; and his hold on the people was such that he could stir them up against anyone who dared oppose his stiff will. But more than that, he was the one who spoke for the gods. He was the agent of those great shadowy powers of sky and earth, fire and water, growth and death and destiny, before which men quailed. Even Carl felt a shiver in his flesh at thought of what might be stooping over the world and listening to this man's words. For the moment, bitter disappointment was lost in a tide of fear, the inbred fear of many generations, and Carl bowed his head in submission.

It was Lenard who laughed, a hard, ringing bark which jerked their attention back to him. "Dalesmen!" he jeered.

Ralph's thick, fair brows drew into a scowl. "What do you mean?" he rumbled.

55

"I mean that living in this fat land has made women of you," said Lenard. "No sooner is one of your people bold enough to seize the only chance you might have—and it was a good thought you had there, boy—than you throw it away in panic fear of gods you've never seen. It'll be no wonder when the Lann kick you out of your homes."

"You'll find how cowardly we are when it comes to battle!" flared Tom.

"Nor are your own folk exactly brave where it comes to the City," murmured Owl. "We, at least, dared to enter the place."

Lenard frowned. "That may be true. But it isn't the City that will decide this—nor are all my warriors afraid of taboos."

Carl leaned forward, seeking that gaunt, brown face out of flickering shadow as if to read a meaning in its lines and scars. "Why are you attacking us?" he asked. "We never harmed you."

"The Lann go where they please," said Lenard haughtily.

"But *why?*"

"It is simple." The prisoner shrugged. "As long as our Doctors remember, we of the north have wrung a scanty living from a harsh and barren land. We have been hunters, herdsmen, small farmers ever at the mercy of cold and rain and blight. We have battled each other to death over what little there was, brother falling on brother like wild dogs. Yet every year more are born, there are more to feed. Meanwhile, it has grown yet colder and stormier; the harvests have been more thin each year. It was too much for men to stand! So we have gathered ourselves and turned the warlike skill we gained from fighting each other against those who hold better lands. That is all. And it is enough!"

"But there is room here," protested Carl. "There are forest tracts which need only be logged off and plowed—"

"So we should come as beggars?" Lenard tossed his head like an angered stallion. "None of that for a warrior people. Nor do I think there is enough room for two such large tribes here, even when you count in the forests. No, there is space for only one tribe to live decently, and we mean to be that tribe."

"And what is your intention, then?"

"Why, we will scatter your armies before us and divide your lands among our men, who will then send for their families. Most of the Dalesmen will have to go, of course; where, I don't know or care. Perhaps you can, in your turn, overrun someone else. Some of your people may be allowed to stay as servants of the Lann. That depends on the will of our Chief, my father." There was scorn in Lenard's voice. "And among the Lann, the Chief is Chief—none of this cumbersome nonsense about voting."

"You speak boldly for a prisoner," said Ralph with dangerous gentleness.

"Why shouldn't I?" Lenard grinned. "I know you won't hurt me. Even if I thought you would, I'm not afraid to die. We're a fighting people, we Lann, and you'll soon find it out."

The army of the Dalesmen was ready to march.

In the two days since Carl's return, scouts had brought word that the Lann host was assembling in full strength well to the north, on the edge of the rugged Scarpian district. It seemed clear that they would move against Dalestown, hoping to seize it. Once they held that fortress, it would be easy for them to reduce whatever outposts were left and bring the whole country to heel. Ralph meant to forestall them, catch them on the border, and defeat them in open combat and drive them north again.

"And what will we do if we win, Father?" asked Carl.

The Chief's golden-bearded face was sober. "I don't know," he said. "They could just go home and wait for another chance. I imagine the best thing for us to do would be to follow up our victory—next summer, or even this winter, but in any case we'll have to wait till after harvest. We can't be really safe till we've brought them into subjection. Yet the thought of being a conqueror leaves a bad taste in my mouth, nor are we a soldier-folk who would be well fitted for such a task." He shrugged. "But let's win the first battle first."

There had been no answer, or only an evasive one, from the small neighbor tribes to whom Ralph had appealed for help. They were afraid to anger the Lann if those should win; and they knew that if the Dalesmen won, they would not be punished for their refusal. Ralph's plea that the northerners would soon gobble them up if the Dales fell had not impressed anyone. It was all too true what Lenard had remarked one day: these loose assemblies of quiet farmers and craftsmen had no idea of war or politics.

Now the Chief stood on the porch of his home in a gray misty dawn, looking at the troop of mounted guards who waited for him in the market square. These sat their horses like statues, lances raised, metal polished, plumes and banners agleam with dew. The Chief was dressed like his guardsmen: a wool tunic under his breastplate of hammered steel, leather cloak and breeches, spurred boots, sword and dagger and signal horn belted at his waist. Carl, Tom, and Owl were more lightly armored, in reinforced bull's-hide cuirasses and flat helmets; they had quivers and long-bows hung from their shoulders, for they, with the other warriors not fully grown, would be archers. Beyond the silently waiting men, a dense and unspeaking throng of women and children and old folk milled about, looking and looking.

Lenard, armored in leather, but without weapons, smiled in thin scorn. This would not have been the farewell given an army by his fierce people. The Lann had been cheered out, and the town had been gay with flags and trophies.

Ralph was taking him along under guard, still hoping to use him as a hostage; but he had given no promise not to try escaping, and none had been asked of him.

Old Rob carried Betty out in his arms. The child's face was still cloudy with dreams, and she smiled sleepily at her father as he lifted her. "Come back soon, Daddy?" she whispered.

"Yes—oh, yes!" He held her very close for a moment. Then he gave her back to Rob, who was weeping silently, and spun on his heel. The plumed helmet, in the crook of his arm, he lifted and set on his head. The nose guard gave his face a sudden, strange, inhuman look. He drew on his gloves and walked rapidly to his horse. Carl squeezed Betty's small, curled-up hand and ran after his father, a stinging in his eyes.

They rode down High Street to the main gate. Folk streamed after them, clutching at the men who went past, waving and crying farewell. *"Good-by, good-by, good-by—the gods be with you— come back!"*

The main army waited beyond the walls. Here there was no such order as the trained guardsmen showed. The men who had come on horses sat together, waiting, and each was equipped with whatever he had brought along, lance and sword and ax slung at rest, armor over plain work-clothes, battered helmets set on shaggy heads. The footmen, who were the bulk of the Dale army, sat or stood as it pleased them, leaning on their pikes and axes, talking among themselves even when the Chief rode up. There was also a train of mule-drawn supply wagons, for Ralph could not plunder the country for food as the Lann did; and three young Doctors were attached to them to guard against sickness and enemy magic. That was all. But that number of men, perhaps five thousand, sprawled far over the valley, hiding the muddy ground and filling the gray air with a murmur of life.

Ralph winded his horn, and certain middle-aged men on horses began to thread through the army, blowing their own signals. These were the shrewd, experienced ones Ralph had chosen to lead the several divisions of his host. Standard-bearers lifted their flags, and slowly, with a vast grumble of movement, the soldiers grouped themselves around their banners.

Ralph and his guardsmen were already under way, trotting down the road to the north, and the great snake of his army uncoiled itself and wound after him. It spilled off the narrow track and into the fields, trampling grain and breaking fences—and no doubt, many a farmstead along the way would be missing a few chickens or a fat pig. But that couldn't be helped. The main thing was that they were moving!

Carl, riding beside his father, looked back as the fog lifted and the day grew warm. The army was a black mass behind, men walking along at an easy pace, riders plodding at their side, wagons rumbling dustily in the rear. Pikes and lances and banners rose and fell with the slow steady movement, the tramp of many feet quivered faintly in the earth, voices and a snatch of song drifted up. It was not a very military sight, but Carl's heart lifted with pride. These were free men!

He stopped his pony, letting it graze while the army went by him. As he looked at the mass of them, he saw that the myriad of faces were the faces of men he knew. John, the farmer, riding beside his sons, caught sight of Carl and hailed him. Willy Rattlehead, grinning at a private joke, juggled three balls in the air as he walked. Sam the Trader, richly clad and burned dark by strange suns, steadied his well-muscled bay mare, which was shying at Willy's juggling balls. Little Jimmy-the-Old, off in worn-out shoes to defend his tiny farm, jumped from the path of the skittish mare. Jack the smith, a hammer carried on one mighty shoulder as his weapon of war, offered to defend little Jimmy-the-Old if he should need it.

Fat Bucko groaned and complained every step of the way, but he kept up with the best. Sly, red-haired Gorda, whom no one called anything but Fox, and his inseparable friend, the big hairy simpleton Joe, gave a loud cheer when they saw Carl. Martun the Hunter, lean and quiet and buckskin-clad, marched with long springlike steps, gaining a yard for every stride. Black Dan from the south, who had settled here years ago and brought six tall sons with him to the wars, walked beside Martun; neither of them talking and both of them in perfect understanding.

Rich and reckless young Dick, on a half-tamed stallion, pretended to thrust with his sword at Carl. But Rogga the farmer, who wanted only to be left in peace and would fight for the privilege, called him back into line; and slow-spoken gentle old Ansy, the carpenter, who liked Carl and who was equally peaceful, nodded his approval to Rogga.

Carl knew them all, them and many others. They were his blood and bone, a part of this wide, green land, and it was as if the Dales themselves, the very earth, were rising in anger to cast out the strangers. Yes, it was a good sight to see—a better sight than a troop of half-savage Lann, for all their skill and courage. Carl felt, suddenly, immensely heartened.

What if the magic of the City had failed him? These men were enough. What if the dead hand of taboo had closed heavily down on that vision of wonder he had seen? There would be others days, other ways. Carl broke into song as he rode back toward his father.

Lenard, mounted between four guards, grinned at him. "You seem pretty confident, my friend," he said.

"I am!" Carl waved his hand at the ranks behind him. "Look there, you. Do you really think these folk, with their hearth-fires at their backs, will yield to you?"

"As a matter of fact, yes." Lenard shook his head. "You've got a lot to learn, Carl. Strength and courage aren't everything. The Lann have that too, and besides that they have the knowledge of war. You might be as strong as, say, a smith, but even so you couldn't do his work because you haven't his training."

"The Dales have beaten off other foes," said Carl hotly.

Lenard smiled and made no reply.

The army held a short rest at noon while the cooks prepared food; then they pushed on. Weariness set in. No more talk and song were heard. The grim, dusty slogging over hills and across streams continued endlessly, and when Ralph, at evening, blew the signal to pitch camp, there was one great sigh of relief.

Fires winked and glowed through an enwrapping night. Sentries paced, yawning, watching the slow wheel of the stars for their time of relief. Ralph studied a map by the dim red light of a dying blaze, and held low-voiced conference with his chiefs. Carl tried to stay awake and listen, but his eyes grew too blurred, and he stretched himself in a blanket and slept.

All the next day the rain poured, and the army grumbled to itself as it splashed in wet misery through the mud of fields and roads. That night, the drums of the Doctors throbbed to drive off fever-devils.

On the third day, Ralph's host entered Scarpia, the wild northern province of his tribe. Here few people dwelt. Only rarely did a lonely cottage rise against a sky of wind-driven clouds, and trees grew thick and gloomy on the rugged backs of steep-sided hills. Crows hovered darkly overhead. Now and again a solitary eagle rode majestic wings above the men, and deer and wild ponies fled as they spied the moving army. Men scrambled up high banks of raw, red earth, forded brawling rivers, crashed their way through tangled underbrush in a roadless land, and many shivered and mumbled spells as they saw the gaunt gray shapes of stones raised long ago by savage woods-runners. But they went on—

Carl was riding with the Chief in midafternoon when a horseman galloped up, mud-splashed and panting, to gasp out his word, ''The Lann are ahead!''

''How far?'' snapped Ralph. Carl's heart leaped wildly and then settled to a high, steady pounding.

''Two, three miles,'' answered the scout. ''They're camped near a big river—thousands of them. They darken the ground!''

''Well—'' Ralph looked grim, then turned to his guards with a smile. ''Let's just keep going, then. Pass the word along.''

Carl could see and almost feel the sudden tension in the men as the report went down their ranks. Eyes looked into eyes, wondering how many more suns they would see, hands tightened on the shafts of weapons, horses sensed the uneasiness in their masters and snorted.

Company commanders blew their horns, and the ragged lines drew together. Outriders spread on either side, ranging the woods which gloomed about the army. Feet broke the dull rhythm of travel and quickened, pressing forward.

Carl glimpsed Lenard, sitting between his guards and watching the Dalesmen prepare. He appeared to be amused.

"They'll know we're coming, Father," said the boy.

"Can't be helped," said Ralph. "We'll just have to reach favorable ground before they attack." For an instant, the hardness of the leader was gone, and he touched Carl's hand with a sudden tenderness. "Be careful, son. Be brave, but be careful."

They thrust ahead, plowing through brush, panting up a long slope of forested hill. The woods ended on its crest and Ralph drew rein. A sunbeam speared through hurrying clouds to touch his armor with fire as he pointed. "The Lann!"

Carl's eyes swept the ground. The ridge went down on a gentler grade here, a long grassy incline broken by clumps of young trees, ending in a broad, level field where the Lann were camped. Beyond that lay the river, a wide watery stretch gleaming like gray iron in the dull, shifting light, trees rising thick on its farther side. On either hand, a mile or less away, the forest marched down to the river on the near side, hemming in the open ground.

The Dalesmen looked first on the Lann warriors. Their tents were pitched on this bank—only a few, for most of those hardy warriors disdained such cover. They swarmed down by the river. It was indeed dark with men and horses, a whirling storm of movement as their horns shrilled command. Banners flying, lance heads hungrily aloft, hideously painted shields and breastplates glistening, bearded faces contorted with battle fury; they were a splendid and terrible sight, and Carl's heart stumbled within him.

Ralph was looking keenly down on them. "Not so many as we," he murmured. "Three or four thousand, I guess—but better trained and equpped, of course. And their Chief can't be so very smart. He let us get this close without trying to stop us, and now we have the advantage of higher ground."

"Why should Raymon fear you?" sneered Lenard. "The Lann can get ready as fast as you can."

Ralph galloped his horse across the front of his army, shouting orders. He had rehearsed his men at Dalestown, and they fell into formation more quickly than Carl had thought they would. But his own eyes were on the man who rode down toward the northerners with a white flag in his hand. Ralph was going to try one last parley. . . .

The rider threw up his arms and tumbled under his suddenly plunging horse. A moment later, Carl heard the faint clang of the bow and the cruel barking laughter of men. The Lann didn't parley—and now they themselves were ready and moving up against the Dalesmen!

CHAPTER 8

Storm from the North

RALPH'S army was drawn up in the formation his people had always used, a double line in the shape of a blunt wedge, with himself and most of his guards at the point. Those in the first rank had axes and swords; behind them, the men slanted long pikes out between the leaders, with their own infighting weapons handy if they should have to step into the place of a fallen comrade. The banners of company commanders were planted at intervals along the lines, whipping and straining in the stiff, damp breeze. Horsemen waited on the flanks, lances lowered and swords loose in the scabbards. On higher ground, spread along the wedge in their own line, were the boys and the oldest warriors, armed with bows and slings. The arrangement was good, tight enough to withstand an attack without crumpling and then move forward against the enemy.

The Lann, Carl saw, were approaching in a compact square of foot soldiers, about half the number of the Dalesmen. Their cavalry, much larger than that of their opponents, waited in a line of restless, tightly held horses near the river. Briefly, Carl thought that his own side had an enormous advantage. A frontal assault of lancers would have shattered itself against pikes and hamstringing swords; in any case, he could not think that cavalry would be of much use on this crowded field. Since almost half the Lann were mounted, it seemed that Ralph had already put that many out of useful action. That was a cheering thought.

And Carl needed cheering. The sight of that approaching line of fiercely scowling strangers brought a cold, shaking thrill along his nerves and muscles. His tongue was thick and dry, his eyes blurred, and something beat in his ears. In moments, now, battle would be joined, his first real battle, and that sun, lowering westward behind windy clouds, might never see him alive again.

The Lann broke into a trot up the hill, keeping their lines as tight as before. A rapid metallic banging began within their square, a gong beating time for their steadily approaching feet, and pipes skirled to urge them on. The red flag of the north flapped on each corner of the formation, bloody against the restless gray heavens. Closer—closer—here they came!

Carl fitted an arrow to the string from the full quiver before him. Tom and Owl stood on either side, their own bows strained, waiting for the signal. The Lann were close, terribly close. Carl could see a scar zigzagging across one square, bronzed face—gods, would the horn never blow?

Hoo-oo-oo!

At the signal, Carl let his arrow fly. The heavy longbow throbbed in his hand. Over the Dale ranks that storm of whistling, feathered death rose, suddenly darkening the sky—down on the Lann! Carl saw men topple in the square, clawing at the shafts in their bodies, and yanked another arrow forth. Fear was suddenly gone. He felt a vast, chill clearness. He saw tiny things with an unnatural sharp vision, and it was as if everything were slowed to a nightmare's dragging pace. He saw the wounded and slain Lann fall, saw their comrades behind them trample the bodies underfoot as they stepped into the front ranks—Zip, zip, zip, give it to them!

"Yaaaah!" Tom was howling as he let fly, his fiery hair blown wild as the lifted banners. Owl fired machine-like, one arrow after the next. Carl had time for a brief wondering as to how he looked, and then the Lann struck.

Swords and axes were aloft, banging against shields, a sudden clamor of outraged iron. Men yelled, roared, cursed as they struck, shields trembled under blows, pikes thrust out and daggers flashed. Carl saw the lines of Dalesmen reel back under the shock, planting feet in suddenly slippery ground, hammering at faces that rose out of whirling, racketing fury and were lost again in the press of armored bodies. He skipped backward, up the hill, seeking a vantage point from which to shoot.

Ralph towered above the battle, smiting from his horse at helmeted heads, lifted arms, snarling faces. The animal reared, hoofs striking out, smashing and driving back. A spear thrust against the Chief. He caught it in his left hand, wrenched it loose, and clubbed out savagely while his sword danced on the other side. A Lann soldier rose yelling under the belly of his horse, and Ralph's spurred heel crashed into his face. Dropping the spear, the Dale chief lifted his horn and blew, long, defiant shrieks that raised answering shouts.

Backed against a thicket, Carl looked over the confusion that boiled below him. The Dalesmen were holding—the Dalesmen stood firm—oh, thank all gods! A sob caught in his throat. He took aim at a mounted piper in the square, and his bow sang and the man staggered in the saddle with an arrow through his shoulder. Mostly Carl was firing blindly into the thick of a mass that swayed and trampled and roared all along the hill.

A spear flew viciously close, plowing into the earth beside him. Arrows were dropping here and there, and stones were flying. The Lann had their own shooting men. Carl growled and planted his legs firm in the grass and shot.

Thunder burst in his head, light flared against a sudden, reeling darkness. He toppled to hands and knees, shaking a head that rang and ached, fighting clear of the night. "Carl! Carl!"

He looked up into Owl's anxious face and climbed unsteadily erect, leaning on the younger boy. "Not much," he mumbled. "Flung stone—my helmet took the blow—" His skull throbbed, but he stooped to pick up his weapons.

Back and forth the struggle swayed, edged metal whistling against armor and flesh, deep-throated shouts and hoarse gasps and pain-crazed screams, the air grown thick with arrows and rocks. Ralph was not in sight—Carl's heart stumbled, then he glimpsed his father's tall form on foot, hewing about him. His horse must have been killed—

Horse! Where were the Lann horses?

Carl grew chill as his eyes ranged past the fight, down the hill to the river. Only the empty tents and the empty trees to be seen. What were two thousand mounted devils doing?

A scream of horns and voices gave him the answer. He looked right and left, and a groan ripped from him. They had come from the woods into which they had slipped. They were charging up the hill and from the side against the Dalesmen's cavalry. He felt the rising thunder of galloping hoofs, saw lances drop low and riders bend in the saddle, and he yelled as the enemy struck.

The impact seemed to shiver in his own bones. Lances splintered against shields or went through living bodies. The inexperienced Dalesmen fell from the saddle, driven back against themselves in a sudden, wild whirlpool. . . . Swords out, flashing, whistling, hacking, rising red!

The Dale foot soldiers had all they could do to stand off the unending Lann press. Meanwhile, their flanks were being driven in, crumpling, horses trampling their own people, warriors speared in the back by lances coming from the rear. Carl fumbled for an arrow, saw that he had used them all, and cursed as he drew his sword and slipped his left arm into the straps of his shield.

The Lann gongs crashed and the Lann pipes screamed in triumph, urging their men on against a wedge that was suddenly breaking up in confusion. Carl saw one of the guards fall, saw Ralph leap into the vacant saddle, and dimly he heard his father's roar: "Stand fast! Stand fast!"

It was too late, groaned the boy's mind. The Dalesmen's host was broken at the wings, forced back against itself by Lann cavalry raging on the flanks and Lann footmen slipping through loosened lines. They were done, and now it was every man for himself.

A couple of enemy horsemen saw the little knot of archers at the thicket, laid lances in rest, and charged. Carl saw them swelling huge, heard the ground quivering under hoofs, caught a horribly clear glimpse of a stallion's straining nostrils and the foam at its mouth and the rider's eyes and teeth white in a darkened, blood-streaked face. He acted without thought, hardly heard himself shouting. "Tom, Owl, get that horse—the legs—"

His own sword dropped from his fingers. The lance head was aimed at his breast, he skipped aside, and it blazed past him. He sprang, clutching at the reins beyond as he had often done to stop runaways. The shock of his own weight slammed back against his muscles. He set his teeth and clung there, and the horse plunged to a halt. Tom's knife gleamed by Carl's feet, hamstringing. The horse screamed, and a dim corner of Carl's mind had time to pity this innocent victim of human madness. Then the Lann warrior was springing lithely from the stirrups, to meet Owl's spear thrust and fall in a rush of blood. The other horse was running riderless, its master sprawled in the grass with a Dale arrow in him.

But the Dalesmen were encircled, trapped, fighting desperately in a tightening ring. Lann were among them, cutting, smiting, riding their foes down. Carl and his little band stood by the thicket looking at a scene of horror.

Light was dimming—gods, was the sun down already? Or . . . had the struggle lasted this long?

"To me, Dalesmen! To me!"

Ralph's deep shout lifted over the clatter and scream of battle. He and the remnants of his guards were gathered around the last Dale banner not fallen to the reddened ground, hewing, driving off the Lann who rushed against them. The Chief winded his horn even as he engaged an enemy horseman, and men lifted weary heads and began to fight a way over to him.

"Come on!" snapped Carl. "All together! Stick close together! We've got to get there!"

They moved away from the thicket in a tight-packed square, perhaps thirty young archers and slingers with swords out. A detachment of Lann foot soldiers came against them. Carl bent low, holding his shield before his body, peering over the top and thrusting. A man attacked, using his own shield to defend himself. Even in the deepening murk, Carl saw the golden ring in the man's nose.

The northern sword clashed against his own steel. He thrust back, hammering at the shield and the helmet, stabbing for the face that grinned at him. He hardly felt the shock of blows on his own metal. Probe—side-swipe—catch his blade on your own, twist it away, straighten your arm and stab for the golden ring—

The man was gone as the fight shifted. Carl was battling someone else. That was war, a huge confusion where men fought strangers that came out of nowhere and were as mysteriously gone. Now there was a shout on his left; another small group of Dalesmen was joining theirs and the Lann melted away.

Ralph's standard flew before them. They came up to him and entered the growing ring of warriors rallying about their Chief. The Lann yelped against that wall of flying steel, dogs attacking a herd of wild bulls. And more Dalesmen made their way over to Ralph, and then more.

The darkness had grown thick. Carl could hardly see the men he fought except as shadows and a gleam of wet metal. His breath was harsh and heavy in dry throat and laboring breast.

Ralph's voice seemed to come from very far away: "All right—now we cut our way free!"

He rode out of the ring, laying about him from the saddle, and his men stumbled after him. They were drawn close together by instinct and the press of the foe, but in the raging gloom there was little need of skill. You struck and took blows yourself and threw your own weight into the mass that jammed against buckling enemy lines.

Ralph and a few guards rode up and down the tattered Dale ranks, smiting at the foe, shouting their own men on, holding together and leading them into the woods. When the trees closed about that great weary retreat, men stumbled and groped a way forward in the utter darkness. For an instant, wild panic beat in Carl. He wanted to run away, run and run and run forever from this place of slaughter, but he heard his father's voice, and a tired steadiness came. He thought dully that without Ralph, there would simply have been a stampede, even if the Dalesmen had somehow managed to escape that trap; the Lann could have hunted them down as hounds hunt down a stag. But the Chief had saved them. He had held his beaten army together and—

Now the fighting had ceased. They fumbled a slow way through brush and trees, down the hill into darkness, but still no Lann confronted them.

Carl knew that the night had saved them. In this thick gloom, with trees and bushes everywhere to hinder movement, the Dalesmen could have stood off whatever came against them and somehow cut a way to safety. The Lann Chief must have realized this and drawn back. They were free.

Free and alive! Carl drew a shuddering breath of the damp night air and a slow feeling of wonder grew in him. He could still move. Blood still ran in his veins. A pattern of shadows and vague light still covered his eyes. He lived, he lived, and it was a heady thing to know.

Weariness and despair came back in a rush. The Dalesmen had escaped with the bulk of their army, yes. But it was a beaten force, streaming home before a victorious enemy, tired and hurt and hopeless. They could not take a stand again. And now the unconquerable Lann would be spilling all over the Dales, with nothing to stop them.

Ralph's voice drifted above the rustle of brush and dragging of feet and hoarse gasping breath of men. A roll of names. He was calling the roll of his guardsmen.

"Ezzeff" — "Here." — "Toom" — "Here." — "Rodge" — "Still alive, Chief."—"Jonathan"—Silence. "Jonathan!"—Silence.

"Where are Torsen and Piggy?"

"Both killed. I saw Piggy go down myself."

Alarm shivered in Ralph's call. The forest muffled his voice. It sounded strangely dead. "But they were guarding Lenard!"

"The Lann must've got him back then."

"Lenard—free again!"

CHAPTER 9

The Broken Ban

MORNING came, chill and gray and hopeless. Men looked wearily about with eyes from which the nightmare of stumbling through dark forest and hills was only slowly lifting.

The army straggled across the rough Scarpian landscape, men walking in small disordered groups. Thickets and ravines hid many from Carl's eyes, but he was sure that the bulk of Ralph's warriors had escaped.

Only a few were very badly wounded, for the retreating Dalesmen had found no chance to rescue comrades in such plight. But all of them were slashed and battered, stiff with dried blood, clothes hanging ragged and dew-wet on exhausted bodies. Not many horses had been saved, and the most hurt rode these. Even Ralph was afoot now, carrying his own torn flag.

Carl's body was one vast, numb ache. His head felt hollow with tiredness, and he staggered a little as he walked. Only now was he becoming really aware of his wounds, a gash across one thigh which Tom had crudely bandaged, a throbbing lump on his head, bruises turning blue and yellow along his arms and breast. Swords and forest thorns had ripped his clothes, the blade at his waist was nicked and blunted with use, the bow was gone and the corselet was heavy on his shoulders.

Owl grinned painfully at his side. One eye was black and

swollen, and he seemed to be short a tooth. "So this," he said, "is the excitement and glory of war! I'll never believe a ballad singer again."

"At least," said Tom slowly, "we're all alive—You and Father and Carl here. Give thanks for small blessings."

Carl thought of those who were dead. He hadn't had time yet to search for all his friends, but he knew that many were gone. Dick, the wild and gay, fat, stanch Bucko, soft-voiced Ansy—he'd never see them again in this world. They were sprawled on the red riverbank where the enemy went hallooing past their sightless eyes, and the sun shone and the wind whispered in long grasses and their kinfolk waited weeping, but they didn't know it.

Dead—dead and defeated.

Ralph was striding toward the brow of a tall hill. He walked stiffly, limping and leaning on his flagstaff, his face a mask of dried blood under the battered helmet, but the wide shoulders were unbowed and morning light struck gold from his hair. When he reached the top, he planted the banner and blew his horn.

Though the cry was feeble, lost in the ringing, echoing reach of hills, the Dalesmen hearkened, and slowly, slowly, they gathered beneath him until their stooped forms hid the dew-glimmering earth. When they were all there, they sat and waited. Ralph's chiefs, such as lived, joined him, and Carl slipped up to stand by his father. But weariness was too heavy on him, and he sat instead, drawing his knees up under his chin and looking forth over the tired, beaten faces of the tribesmen.

Ralph spoke, filling his lungs so that most of the army could hear and pass the word along: "We haven't been pursued yet, and I think the Lann would have caught up to us by now if they cared to. So most likely they're letting us go, not thinking us worth the trouble of another fight."

"We aren't," said a man, grinning without humor.

"They'll learn otherwise!" Ralph folded his arms and looked defiantly around. "We've lost a battle, yes, but we haven't lost the war. Not if we stick together and fight on."

"We're done for, Chief, and you know it." Another man stood up near the crest of the hill, a gray-haired farmer with a sullen anger in his eyes. "Best we scatter, go to our homes, and flee south while we can."

A low mumble went through the close-packed warriors, heads nodded and hands dropped slackly to the grass.

Ralph lifted his voice to a shout: "That's coward's advice, Bilken, and I'd not have looked for that from you."

"I lost one son at that battle," answered the farmer. "Why should I lose the rest—for nothing?"

"But it's not for nothing!" cried Ralph. "It's for our homes and wives and children, for freedom, for our very lives. Where can we go as the trickling remnants of a broken people? Who will receive us? What will we do when the Lann swallow the next tribe, and the next, and the one after that? Become their slaves? Cut their wood and draw their water and clean their barns? Kneel in the mud when a horseman goes by? Was it for this that our fathers cleared the woods and plowed the land and fought the savages? Has their blood turned to water in our veins?"

"We can't fight," croaked Bilken. "We've nothing to fight with."

"Yes, we have. We have other weapons. We have other horses. One night's rest will give us new strength. We have Dalestown, whose walls have never been stormed. We have our bare hands, if need be!" Ralph shook the banner, and its golden field uncurled in the dawn breeze. "Are we still the Dalesmen or are we field mice running before a scythe? By all the gods, I'll fight alone if I must!"

"They'll coop us up inside the walls while they burn our homes," cried a voice.

"Nonsense! They won't burn that which they themselves want to take over. And even if they do, what of it? Your homes are lost anyway if you flee. But if we win, there is always more wood and stone for building. There's always the land."

Ralph waved an arm at the hills and trees that stretched to a far blue horizon. "There's always the land," he repeated. "Without it, we are nothing—woods-runners, beggars, homeless and hopeless tramps. These are the Dales, and while we hold them we are strong and rich and happy. While we fight for our earth, it will give us of its strength. Dalesmen, free men, will you give away your birthright?"

It struck home. Carl saw a new light in dulled eyes, saw fingers close on the hafts of weapons and men rise to their feet. A ragged cheer lifted slowly, pulsing out like the golden flag that waved overhead. The farmer Bilken nodded grudgingly and sat down. When it came to a vote, there were few who said "No."

Truly Ralph was a leader of men!

But Carl saw that this hope was hollow. What, indeed, could be done against a foe who had already smashed their finest power, a foe who must even now be spilling out across the wide land and bringing terror where he went? The Dalesmen could retreat inside their walls, perhaps, but then what could they do? Wait for starvation, or sally forth to die?

He shook his head, feeling weariness overwhelm him. But even then a resolution was gathering in his mind.

The army rested most of that day. Ralph commandeered horses from the nearest farm and sent men galloping out. One would bear word of ruin back to Dalestown, one or two would try to spy on the enemy movements, the rest would pass a message to the scattered homesteads of the tribe and let them carry it farther: retreat to town, we are beaten and must draw into our shell.

But many a lonely farm, thought Carl, would already have received that word from the fire and sword of the Lann.

He spoke to his father a little, as they sprawled in the grass waiting for a sleep which would not come: "What do you hope to do? Do you really believe we can fetch victory, even now?"

"I don't know," said Ralph dully. "It may be that we can, somehow, by some miracle. Or it may be that we will give the Lann so much trouble that they'll be willing to bargain and take less than everything. That would at least give us a breathing space. Or it may well be that we will go down to utter defeat. But even then—" He looked sternly up. "Even then, Carl, we'll have fought like Dalesmen!"

The boy made no answer. Privately, he wondered if there was not something blind in this courage. To go down fighting—well, it left a brave memory, but if it gained nothing except the slaughter of many men, it seemed useless. The best leader was one who gained victory with as little bloodshed as could be. Yes, as little on *both* sides as possible.

In the afternoon, Ralph summoned his men, and they started the weary trek homeward. There would be little food under way, for the supply wagons were lost and the farms on the route could not help so many. The Chief had foragers ranging widely, who would bring in as much as they could, but even so it would be a cold and hungry march. He drove his followers unmercifully, forcing stiff bodies to a cruelly fast pace and taking curses without reply. They had to get inside the walls as fast as could be managed, for, if the Lann fell on a host weakened with emptiness, it could be butchery.

Carl walked beside Tom and Owl as before. He had become very close to these brothers since they followed him to the City. The days had been so full that it seemed they had known each other for many years. Tom's quiet thoughtfulness, Owl's unfailing good humor—he needed them, and they in turn looked to him as a leader. It was good to have friends.

He spoke to them now, as the slow miles dragged by: "You know we haven't much chance. We can't say so out loud, for everyone's too downhearted already, but it's true."

"Well," shrugged Owl, "it might be fun being a landless gypsy."

"That's not so!" flared Tom. "It's right what the Chief said. Without the land, we are nothing."

"Um-m-m—yes—can't say I fancy sleeping in the open all my life, and working for someone else to earn bitter bread. But what can we do about this?"

Carl said softly: "We can return to the City."

"What?" They stared at him, open-mouthed.

"Not so loud!" Carl glanced nervously about him. The nearest group of men was several yards off, and they trudged unnoticing ahead, faces blank with weariness. But the Doctors—you never knew when a Doctor might be somewhere, listening.

He went on, rapidly: "You know the powers of the ancients are locked in the time vault. You know Ronwy is our friend and will help us, and that he has some understanding of the old—science. If we can sneak away from this army tonight and make our way to the City, we can carry back the lightning to drive off our enemies!" Carl's eyes burned with a feverish eagerness. "We can—*learn*."

"Taboo!" whispered Tom. "The gods—"

"If the gods really cared about that taboo, they'd have knocked us over the first time we broke it. They'd never have let the witch-men live in the ruins."

"But the witch-men have magic powers—" stuttered Owl.

"Bah!" Carl felt strength rising in him even as he spoke. "You saw those witches yourself. You know they're just frightened outcasts, trading on our fears. I—" He tumbled the words out before he should have time to be afraid. "I wonder if there are any gods at all—if they aren't just another story."

Tom and Owl shrank from him. But no lightning struck.

"*Someone* must have made the world," said Tom at last, his voice trembling.

"Yes, yes. The great God that the time vault spoke of—that I could believe in. But the other gods—well, if they exist, they're not very big or very smart. Why, in all the stories, they do things no child would care to do." Carl dropped the subject. "That doesn't matter now, though. It's just that I'd rather listen to Ronwy, who's spent his life among the ancient works, than to Donn, who's never been inside the taboo circle. And Ronwy says there's nothing to fear and much to gain."

"But it's Donn who'll have you put to death," said Owl.

Carl grinned. "When I come back with Atmik's Power in my hand? I'd like to see him try!"

Tom shook his red head. "It's a big thing you want to do. And we're young yet."

"This won't wait till we grow up; meanwhile, there's no one else to do the job. I tell you, boys, that vault has *got* to be opened, opened to the Dales—no, by Atmik, to all the world!" Carl's voice dropped. "What have we to lose? Sure, it's a slim chance, but you know that there's no other chance at all. I'm going there. Do you want to come along?"

"If I had any sense," said Owl, "I'd report this to your father, and he'd tie you up till this madness is past."

Carl's heart grew leaden.

"But since I'm not very sensible," smiled Owl, "why, I'll just have to tag along after you."

"Good lad!" Carl slapped his back, and Owl winced.

Tom shook his head. "You're crazy, both of you," he said. Then, with sudden firmness: "But just so nobody can say I hung back from a dangerous mission, count me in."

Yes—it was good to have friends!

The army marched on past sunset, through the long summer twilight and on under starlight and a thin sickle of moon. It was long after dark when Ralph called a halt.

Even then there was much to do. The men had to be disposed on the sides of a hill where they could make a stand in case of attack. Sentries had to be posted and scouts assigned to ride around the area. Foragers trickled in with whatever they had been able to beg or steal, and a cooking fire blazed low under a shielding rock. Here they had good fortune: on a near-by farm, deserted by its owners, two cows were found and led to the camp for butchering. Each man had only a taste, though many were so tired that they went directly to sleep without waiting for their ration.

Carl himself dozed off where he lay under a tree. When he awoke, it was near midnight and the Dalesmen slept around him. Wherever he looked, dark forms sprawled on the ground and a low muttering of sleep lifted to the glittering stars. The fire's last coals were a dull-red eye against the massive darkness of the hill.

He got up, stretching stiff sinews. He was cold and wet and hungry. His wounds ached and his skin was sticky with sweat and dirt. But the rising excitement thudded in veins and nerves, driving out such awareness even while it sharpened his senses. Gently, he shook Tom and Owl awake where they lay beside him.

"We'll have to swipe horses," he breathed. "They're hobbled over there. Easy now, 'ware the sentries."

Slowly, patiently, the three crawled on their bellies toward the shadowy forms of animals. They had to cross a guardsman's beat. Carl lay in tall wet grass, hearing the sigh of wind and the distant creaking song of crickets. Looking upward, he saw the man go past, a dim sheen of metal against the Milky Way. Snakelike, he writhed over the line.

Metal chinked on stone. "Who goes there?" shouted the watcher.

The boys lay stiff, hardly breathing, trying to still even the clamor of their hearts.

After a moment, the warrior decided that it had been nothing and trudged on his way. Carl slid over to the nearest horse. He could hear it cropping grass, and it tried to move away as he approached.

"Steady," he whispered. "So, so, boy, easy." He rose beside the animal and stroked its neck. If only it wouldn't whinny!

Gently he bridled it, using a length of rope to make a hackamore. This would have to be bareback too. But it wasn't far to the City, perhaps a day and a half through woods. Once they got away, the boys would hardly be trailed; three missing horses at daybreak would be set down to thieves, and in the disordered mass of the army, it might well be evening before Carl himself and his followers were missed.

The others joined him, leading their mounts from the sleeping camp. When they were well away, they sprang to the horses' backs and rode westward.

CHAPTER 10

Vengeance of the Gods

THE City brooded under a hot, cloudless heaven, without sign of life. But the notion shuddered in Carl that it was a *waiting* stillness, and he fought to drive the superstition from his mind.

"There she is," said Owl. He sat his horse in the shade of a tree, whose leaves hung unstirring in the breathless quiet, and looked past the wrecked outer buildings to the desolated splendor of the towers. "And now what do we do?"

Carl wiped the sweat from his face. "We go to the time vault," he replied as steadily as possible.

"The witch-men won't be happy about that," warned Tom.

"Then they'll have to be unhappy," snapped Carl. "We've got their Chief on our side, at least."

Stones rattled as they rode down an empty street. Once a lithe form went bounding across their path, a weasel, and once there was a flock of crows which flew blackly overhead, otherwise nothing but the stillness of dead centuries. In spite of the summer heat, Carl felt a chill tingle. It was hard to keep calm reason when violating the home of the gods. He remembered a saying of Donn's: "When the gods are angered, their revenge is not always swift death. They often choose the more cruel punishment of unending bad luck."

But that was wrong, Carl reminded himself. If the idols of the Dalesmen were no more than wood and stone, then only the great

God of the ancients could really be alive—and *he* would be more just than the powers of earth and air and fire.

"Down this street," he pointed. "We needn't enter the section where the witches live. The important thing is to hold the time vault."

Tom nodded. "That's right. Three of us, between those two high walls leading to it, could stand off an army—for a while."

It was easy to get lost here, winding between endless heaps of brick and overgrown foundations. Several times Carl had to find a long avenue at whose end he could see the great towers. His woodsman's eye had noted their relation to the vault when he was last there, and—

"Up ahead!"

Carl reined in at Owl's shout, and his sword rasped from its sheath. A dozen witch-men stood with bows and spears in front of the horse-skull sign. They were small and scrawny and unarmored, but there was a terrible grimness on their faces.

A noise behind made Carl look around, and he saw another party of the City dwellers coming from around a corner. The boys were in the middle of a street between the roofless, clifflike walls of two giant buildings—trapped! Trapped and taken!

"Let's get away," muttered Owl. "If we charge those fellows on horseback—their line'll break—"

"Do not move!" The voice was shrill. Carl, who had heard that panicky note in other cries, knew that the speaker was made dangerous by fear. He would kill at the first sign of fight. And there were many drawn bows and poised spears—

Slowly, with vast care, the boy clashed his sword back into the scabbard. "We come in peace," he said. "Where is Ronwy?"

"The Chief is on his way." The man who spoke was sullen, his eyes smoldered on them behind the arrow he held leveled on Carl's heart. "You will wait."

"Is this how you treat your guests?" asked Owl.

"You are not guests. You are prisoners. Dismount!"

The boys climbed to the ground and stood glaring at the witch-men. But there was nothing to do, nothing at all.

Someone was pounding a drum, and the muffled thunder echoed from wall to staring wall. Presently an answer came, beating from far away. The dwellers were summoning others. Carl found a shady spot and sat down. Owl joined him, grinning maliciously. "It'll get mighty tiring to stand holding a drawn bow," he remarked.

"Be quiet!" snapped the leader.

Presently Ronwy came, with a troop of armed witch-men after him. The tall old Chief pushed through the lines of his people and hurried to take Carl's hands in his own. "What have you done?" he cried. "What have you done?"

"Nothing, yet," said Carl. "We simply rode in, which is against Dale but not City law, and suddenly we were captured."

There were tears running along Ronwy's furrowed cheeks. "The men were afraid you'd come prowling back," he said. "They planted guards near the vault to ambush anyone that came. I couldn't stop it."

"If you were a proper Chief," said the patrol leader, "you wouldn't have wanted to stop it."

"Be still!" shouted Ronwy. "I am Chief of the City even now. These boys go with me."

"They do not," replied the leader coldly. "They're our prisoners, and I say kill them before they work further mischief."

"And bring the wrath of the Dalesmen down on us?"

The leader's laugh was a harsh bark. "What would the Dalesmen have to say? These young snoops have broken tribal taboo, as you well know. In any case, it isn't the Dalesmen who matter any longer, it's the Lann, and they'll be pleased to get the heads of these fellows."

"Why are you doing this?" asked Carl. "What have we done to hurt you?"

"You came to enter the vault of devils," snarled the leader. "Don't deny that. You headed straight for it. You'd bring down the wrath of the gods on us by your meddling—to say nothing of the Lann. Only your deaths will lift the curse."

A mumble of agreement came from the ragged, sooty figures that hemmed in the captives.

Ronwy stepped forth, tall and lean and angry. His old voice rolled out with a new power: "If you kill these lads, you'll have worse than that to face!" he shouted. "I'm still the Chief of the City. I still have loyal followers. Furthermore, I'm the greatest witch in this tribe. The powers of the Doom are in me. I'll curse you with plague and ruin and the glowing death."

That brought them shuddering back. But some shook their fists and cried that the gods would protect the pious and that Ronwy's sorceries were taboo. For a moment it looked as if that milling throng would begin to fight itself—knives were coming out, spears were lowered. Carl's hand stole to the haft of his sword. There might be a chance to cut a way out of such a riot and escape.

Ronwy and his rival strode among the men, yelling orders and cuffing heads, and a slow calm grumbled back into the tribe. Argument went hotly on, while the boys listened in the dark knowledge that their own lives hung on the outcome. But even in that desperate moment, Carl had to admire Ronwy. The old Chief had little power under the law, and few who would back him up, but his tongue was swift and subtle. He fought with words like a skilled swordsman with flickering blade, and, in the end, he won a compromise. The prisoners would be held for a while, unharmed, until their fate could be decided; and in no case would they be executed until word had been received whether Ralph—or the Lann—cared to ransom them.

"I'm sorry I couldn't do more for you," whispered Ronwy. "But I'll keep trying."

Carl managed to squeeze the old man's trembling hand. "You did splendidly, sir," he answered softly.

Disarmed, the boys were marched to the area of towers. A small ground-floor room in one had been turned into the City jail: a few straw ticks on the floor, a jug of water, a basin, and a door of heavy wooden bars. They were shoved inside. A lock snapped shut as the door thudded closed, and a spearman sat down under a tree to watch them.

"Well," said Owl after a long silence, "we found a vault of sorts."

Tom looked grimly out through the bars. "Helpless!" he said between his clenched teeth. "Like animals in a cage—helpless!"

Day dragged into night. Once the door was opened, and a silent woman gave them some bowls of food. The life of the City went by in the street, folk on their various errands; many spat in the direction of the jail. With darkness there came silence, and presently the captives slept.

They woke with dawn and sat staring at each other. Finally Carl spoke, awkwardly, "I'm sorry I got you into this."

"It's all right," said Tom. "We didn't have to come along."

"What will we do?" asked Owl.

"Nothing," said Tom.

The morning waxed. They were given breakfast and then left alone. The guard was changed, another man sat yawning outside the prison. A terrible bitterness grew in Carl, and he vowed that never again, if he lived, would he keep an animal behind bars.

Late in the morning the boys heard shouts far away. They crowded to the door and strained against it, staring out at blank walls across the street. The guard rose, hefting his spear and peering warily about him.

"Rescue?" cried Owl hopefully.

"I doubt it," said Tom. "I don't think the gods are done with punishing us."

A scream rang out somewhere, and the sound of trampling hoofs, and a man's laugh like wild dogs baying. Carl stiffened in a sudden terror. He knew that laughter.

Hoo-oo-oo!

A horn was blowing, and now the rattle of iron swept near. Three women ran down the street, clutching children to them, screaming. The guard outside the jail ran from sight toward the noise of battle.

"Someone's fighting their way into the City!" yelled Tom.

Carl gripped himself, biting back fear. His knuckles were white where he clutched the bars of the jail. He tried to shake them—useless, useless. He was locked in here and there was nothing he could do.

"Hold fast! Drive them back!"

It was the voice of the patrol leader who had wanted to kill him, and Carl had to admit the man was brave. Swords were banging, a horse neighed, a man screamed.

Backing down the street came a thin line of witch-men. They bore weapons in shaking hands, and many were bleeding from wounds. Even as Carl watched, a bow thrummed and a City dweller toppled with an arrow in him, coughing and clawing.

"All right, men—ride 'em down!"

Lenard!

The horsemen of Lann came like a whirlwind, lances at rest, swords flashing free, plumes and mantles streaming in their thunderous passage. They struck the witch-line with a roar, and it broke before them.

Hewing, hewing, the Lann rode through that boiling tide of men. The City folk turned to run. A mounted warrior galloped after them, laughing aloud. The battle swept on out of sight.

"Lenard," groaned Carl.

The noise of fighting grew more distant. There could be only one end to that struggle, even if the Lann were outnumbered. The unwarlike City men could not stand before the determined, ruthless onslaught of trained warriors.

"But this is taboo for them," gasped Tom.

"Not any longer, it seems." Owl skinned his teeth in a mirthless grin. "They'll simply chase the witches into the forest. And then what do we do, Carl?"

"I don't know," said the Chief's son dully. "I just don't know."

They paced the cell, waiting. Shadows crawled over the street. A crow settled on one of the sprawled bodies, but flapped heavily skyward when a wounded man groaned and stirred.

It seemed ages before hoofs were again ringing in the stillness. The Lann troops rode into sight and drew rein. There were only a score or so, but it had been enough.

Lenard edged his horse over to the prison. "So here you are," he said. "Hello, Carl."

He was in full battle dress, corselet and boots and spiked helmet, and a red cloak swinging from his shoulders and a tunic of rich blue Dale weave covering his lean, muscular body. The dark face split in a wolfgrin. "Bulak, Janzy, get that door open," he ordered.

Two men dismounted and attacked the lock with their battle-axes. It shivered apart and the door creaked wide. "Come on out," said Lenard.

The boys stumbled forth, blinking in the sunlight. Lance heads came down to point ominously at their breasts. Looking around, Carl saw that one elderly man in a red robe was with the troop, and that Ronwy stood by Lenard's bridle.

"Ronwy!" choked Carl.

"I couldn't leave," said the old Chief. "They drove my people into the woods, but I couldn't leave our City."

"I wouldn't've let you, anyway," interrupted Lenard. "According to Carl's story, you're the one who knows how to make those things in the time vault work."

"The time vault!" Carl looked with horror at the Lann prince.

The long, lean head nodded. "Certainly. If the powers of the

Doom would work for you, I don't see why they shouldn't work for us." With a savage gleam of eyes: "We'll be lords of the world if that's right!"

"This place is taboo," bluffed Ronwy desperately. "The gods will be angry with you."

"As a matter of fact," said Lenard, "the Lann—at least, that tribe of the confederation to which I belong—have no taboos on ancient works. Many are frightened of them, but they aren't actually forbidden. I suppose," he added thoughtfully, "that it's because in our home territory we have nothing to forbid. There are none of the old Cities left, only great cratered ruins. So I gathered these bold men here, who'd follow me to storm Sky-Home itself, and with my father's agreement we came to ransack that vault. I took along a Doctor, Kuthay there—" he gestured at the man in the red robe— "to take off any evil spells we might find." His contemptuous smile showed that it had only been to quiet any fears his men might have, and that he himself had no belief in ancient curses. The grin flashed on his new captives. "But I didn't expect to find you here too. Welcome, boys, welcome!"

"I don't know anything really," quavered Ronwy. "I can't make any of those machines work."

"You'd better learn in a hurry, then," said Lenard grimly. "Because if you don't show me some results, all four of you will be killed. Now—off to the time vault—march!"

CHAPTER 11

The Gods Are Angry

THE mounted men reined in before the horse's skull and sat staring between the walls at the high gray cube within. An uneasy mutter went from mouth to bearded mouth, eyes flickered in hard, sun-darkened faces, and hands touched lucky charms. The horses seemed to know the uncertain fear stirring in their masters and stamped restless feet. Plainly the Lann were afraid of the old magic, in spite of Lenard's proud words.

"We're going in," said the northern prince. His voice was oddly flat in the brooding, flimmering silence.

"These places are cursed," mumbled a warrior.

"We've the power of our own gods with us," snapped Lenard.

"Our gods are far away in the north," answered the man.

"Say not so." The old Lann Doctor, Kuthay, took a small iron box from his robe, and the men bent their heads to it. "I have with me the House of Jenzik, and the god himself is in it."

He lifted his hands and broke into a chant. Its high-pitched singsong shivered dully back from the ancient ruins. Carl listened closely, but could make out only a few words; it must be in the old language itself, which had changed greatly since the Doom. When he was through, Kuthay put the box carefully back inside his red garments and said matter-of-factly, "Now we're guarded against whatever spells may be here. Come."

"Wait outside," Lenard ordered his men. "Bulak and Toom—" he nodded to two scarred warriors who had shown no fear—"come with us, the rest mount guard. We won't be in there past sundown."

He swung to the ground. "Lead us in, Ronwy," he said.

Slowly, trembling a little, the old chief began picking his way through the thorny brush and between the heaps of brick and glass. Lenard followed with Kuthay, then the boys; Bulak and Toom, with weapons in hand, came last.

There was a rustle and a rattle and a blur of movement. Lenard swore as the rattlesnake struck. Its fangs sank harmlessly into the thick sole of his boot, and he crushed it with the other foot.

"Are you sure the curse is gone?" asked Carl with grim amusement.

The two warriors were shaken, and old Kuthay had gone white. But Lenard's answer barked angrily forth: "A snake can be anywhere. And this one did no harm, did it? If that's the best the guardians of the vault can do, we're safe."

As they came to the entrance, he pointed to the inscription above it. "What does that say?" he asked. Carl remembered what travelers had long told, that none of the northerners could read.

"Time vault," said Ronwy. He turned solemn eyes on his captors. "It is time itself, and all the ghosts and powers of a past that is not dead, only sleeping, which are locked in here. Enter at your peril."

"Bluff!" snorted Lenard.

The door creaked open under Ronwy's touch. Darkness gaped below. "Go ahead," ordered the prince. "If there are deathtraps inside, they'll get you first."

They fumbled a way down the stairs into the cool night of the cellar. Ronwy felt his way to the table where he had candles and gave one to Lenard. The Lann prince struck fire with flint and steel to light it, and a yellow glow spilled forth over the dusty cases and machines. Lenard's breath sucked in between his teeth and something of the holy fire of wisdom-hunger grew in his eyes as he stared about him. "So this is the vault," he whispered.

He lit other candles until the shadows retreated to the corners and waited huge and threatening. Bulak and Toom posted themselves at the foot of the stairs, looking about with awe-struck vision. Kuthay's lips moved in a voiceless chant. Lenard prowled about among the racks, touching a model here and a book there with fingers that trembled ever so faintly. Carl went over to the bronze plaque and read its appeal again. Tears blurred his eyes.

"What is this?" Lenard touched a thing of metal plates and levers. "An instrument of torture?"

"It is a printing press," said Ronwy tonelessly. "They used it to make books, so that all could learn what was known."

"Bah!" Light and shadow slid across Lenard's savage face, etching it against the shuddering gloom. "What can we use for war?"

"There were no weapons here," said Ronwy. "It was war that destroyed the ancients, and the man who created the vault did not want to raise that devil again."

"I think you're lying." Lenard slitted his eyes. "Carl! Where are the weapons?"

"I don't know of any," said the boy. "Ronwy tells the truth."

"If I put your hands into this—printing press—and crushed them, you might remember."

"What good would that do you?" Ronwy straightened, strangely majestic. "You can't wring facts from us that we don't have."

"There must be something here that can be used in battle," snapped Lenard. "Otherwise Carl wouldn't have had the idea."

"There is—wisdom, knowledge, yes," said Ronwy. He stroked his white beard. "There are no tools of war here, but there are the means of making some."

"What? What can you do?"

The old man went over to a set of shelves where dusty bottles were racked, one beside the other. On his last visit, Carl had not been able to read the legends engraved on the glass. They had been letters and numbers forming no words, and he had thought they were magical signs. Ronwy had told him that they were merely symbols for various substances, and that certain old books— chemistry texts, he called them—had explained these and had told what the substances in combination would do.

"I can make certain things," said the witch-chief, so quietly that his voice was almost lost in the heavy gloom. "For example, from what is in these flasks I can brew a magic potion which men can eat. Thereafter they are invulnerable. No metal can pierce their skins, no stone or club can bruise them, no poison can hurt them. Will that be enough?"

Carl's body jerked, and a wave of sickness swept through him.

Had Ronwy turned traitor? Was he really going to aid these robbers?

Lenard's eyes flamed. "Yes, that will do—for a beginning!" he said. His voice rang forth, triumphant: "An army which cannot be hurt—oh, yes, that will do!"

Even Bulak and Toom started forth, with greed in their faces.

"One moment," said Kuthay shrewdly. "If this is so, why have you not made the City-folk, or yourself at least, invulnerable?"

Ronwy smiled wearily. "This place and its magic is taboo for us," he answered. "My people would have nothing to do with it, and if I used it on myself they would cast me out. Furthermore, the thing is dangerous. There will be devils raised which may break loose, and it angers the gods when men thus take divine powers."

Bulak and Toom shrank back toward the stairs.

"Go ahead," said Lenard coldly. "I'll risk the devils and the gods."

"I need someone to help," said Ronwy. "Carl, will you?"

"No," said the boy. "No, you turncoat."

"Go ahead and help him," ordered Lenard. "You know a little more than any of the rest of us about this." He laid a hand on the hilt of his sword. "Or must I have you—no, not you, but your friends—put to torture?"

Sullenly, Carl went over to the witch-chief. Lenard and Kuthay joined their men at the door, beckoning Tom and Owl over to them.

Ronwy's old hand shook a little as he took down one of the bottles. This one had words on it, besides the chemical symbols, but Carl could not understand them: GUNPOWDER (BLACK). Then he remembered that "guns" were the lightning throwers of legend, and despite himself he shivered.

"This is all the vault has," sighed Ronwy. "But we'll have to use it all. Carl, find me a bowl."

The boy searched through a stack of apparatus until he found a large one. As he brought it back, Ronwy's lips touched his ear and the chief whispered: "I'm trying to trick them."

A surging gladness went through Carl. He held his face tight, not daring to look toward the Lann who stood watching.

Ronwy opened the bottle and spilled the black grains into the bowl. Again he had a chance to murmur. "They may kill us. Shall I go on?"

Carl nodded, ever so faintly.

Ronwy searched for other flasks. Meanwhile, he began to chant, his high, thin voice echoing in a sawtoothed wail that brought gooseflesh even to Carl's skin. Kuthay, a black shadow against the dimly sunlit doorway, lifted the House of Jenzik against magic.

"In the name of Atmik, and the Cloud, and the blue-faced horseman who sowed the glowing death across wasted fields, ten thousand devils chained and raging to be free, by the Doom and the darkness, I conjure you, ancient Rebel, child of night, out of the lower depths—"

"Some more bowls, Carl. Spread the black powder in half a dozen."

Ronwy unstoppered another flask and shook some blue crystals into one bowl. Into another he put a white substance marked *NaCl* but seemingly common salt, and into a third some purplish-black stuff. *"Nee-wee-ho-hah-nee-yai. Atmik, Atmik!"*

A hurried whisper: "Carl, I hope to frighten them from the vault so that they won't dare use its real powers—"

Mumble of witch-chant, rattle of earthenware. *"Hoo-hoo-hoo! Rise, all Powers of night and death and horror, rise to me now!"*

Ronwy handed Carl a copper tube. "Tamp some of the black powder into this. When it is full, find a stopper and close one end tightly."

He stood making gestures, tall and gaunt and unhumanly stiff, a shudder of yellow light and moving darkness across his lined face, eyes burning. When Carl handed him the tube, he had a chance for another whisper: "I don't know what they'll do even if we succeed. I can only hope to frighten them from the City." Loudly: "O almighty gods of earth and sky, fire and water, summer and white winter, be not angry with us. Loose not the devils which are your hounds against us."

Lenard's voice came, not unshaken. "If it's that dangerous, maybe we'd better forget it."

"I can't stop now," said Ronwy tightly. "The Powers are already raised, now we must chain them. I hope we can! *Yah-wee-nay-hah-no-nee!*"

Bulak and Toom cowered behind Kuthay, who held the House of Jenzik aloft in trembling hands.

Ronwy took a length of coarse twine, put it in the open end of the powder tube, and sealed that end with tight-packed clay. He had his own materials and crude apparatus in the vault, which he had used for many years in trying to fathom the secrets here. "Gods of the great world, be not angry!"

"When is it ready?" Lenard's voice was becoming the snarl of a frightened dog.

"Soon, soon. Then or never." Ronwy placed the open bowls on the floor and laid the tube beside them. He took a candle in one hand.

"Now," he said solemnly, his tones echoing as if a ghost spoke with him from the moving shadows, "comes the release of that which we have raised. There will be fire and a stench of devils—bear yourselves bravely, for the devils are like hounds and fly at the throat of anyone who is afraid."

That, thought Carl, was a masterly touch. For how could the Lann help being frightened in their hearts? He himself was cold with sweat, and his heartbeat was loud in his ears.

"Atmik, arise!" Ronwy plunged the candle into the first bowl.

A flame sheeted up, hissing, throwing a terrible death-blue glare on walls and faces and the crouching secret machines. A warrior cried out. Ronwy shook his head so that the long white beard flew wildly.

"Don't be afraid!" he shouted. "It is death to be afraid!"

He lit the next bowl, and the flame was a hard brassy yellow. A choking, stinging smoke of fumes roiled through the vault.

"I smell fear!" screamed Ronwy, and the echoes rolled back, *"Fear, fear, fear. . . ."* He lit the third bowl, and the fire was red.

"Blood, blood!" Ronwy's voice trembled. "The sign of death. Someone here is going to die."

"I go!" Toom whirled and rushed up the stairs. Lenard roared at him. The flames rushed higher. Ronwy lit the last bowl, and it burned green.

"The green of mold and death," he wailed. "The green of grass on the graves of men. Atmik, Atmik, go back! All gods help us!"

He touched the candle to the twine fuse of the copper tube.

"Let the torch of the gods be lit to aid us," he quavered.

A dim red spark glowed, eating inward.

"The torch will not light—the gods have turned their faces from us—now flee for your lives!" Ronwy stumbled toward the door. Bulak howled and followed Toom up the stairs. Kuthay came after, then Tom and Owl, as frightened as their captors. The flames sheeted in the vault—blue and yellow and red and green, hard terrible light of wrath—and pain stabbed in lungs as the fumes swirled through the chamber.

Lenard spread his legs and raised his sword. "I'm staying!" he cried, and even then Carl had to admire his courage.

"Stay, then—and die!" Ronwy brushed past him, Carl on his heels. A moment later Lenard came. He had dropped his sword, and the breath sobbed in his throat.

A bang came thundering to earth, a spurting fire and the crash of echoes, as the tube blew up. A hot metal splinter whizzed savagely from the doorway.

Lann horses plunged in terror. "We're getting out of here!" screamed a man.

"No! Wait!" Lenard grasped at bridles, shouting, cursing. "See, the fires are dying down there. It is over!"

"Death, death!" wailed Ronwy eerily. "The glowing death is on us."

Bulak hefted his ax and glared at Lenard. "We're going," he snapped. "There are ghost and devils loose here."

"No!" bellowed the prince.

"Yes!" Old Kuthay stood forth, shaking in his red robes, his face gray and sweating. "Even Jenzik could not halt the powers of the Doom. It will take our greatest magic and many sacrifices to lift the curse that is on us now, and the gods—our gods, too—won't stand for more meddling." He lifted the iron box. "In the name of Jenzik the High, I declare this place, vault and City and accursed witchfolk, taboo. Taboo forever! And may death be swift for him who breaks the law."

Lenard stood like a bear at bay, snarling into the faces of his men. "Cowards!" he yelled. "Oh, crawling cowards and traitors!"

"We're going," grunted Toom. "We'll follow you anywhere else, but if you want to lead us, you'll come along now."

"Well—well—" Lenard fought for self-control. Slowly, an iron smile twisted his lips. "Well, all right. We can take the Dales without need of magic."

He mounted his horse and gestured to the prisoners. "Come along," he snapped. "You can still be useful, dead if not alive."

"Not the old one." Kuthay pointed to Ronwy. "He is full of the Doom. There is no luck in him."

"Leave him, then. Take the boys along, at least, and let's get out of here."

Ronwy stood for a long time, staring after the Lann and their prisoners. Then he sighed and turned back to the vault. When he came in, he went anxiously about to see if the explosion had done any harm. Finally he stopped before the bronze plaque, and his thin fingers touched it.

"You saved us," he whispered, and there were tears glimmering in his eyes. "You saved us. But at what cost?"

CHAPTER 12

"Ride to Dalestown!"

THE three boys, lent extra horses which the troop had taken along, rode untied, but they were carefully watched by their captors. It was a swift, trotting journey until they were well away from the City; then the pace slowed and the men began to breathe more easily.

Carl looked about him at the great sweep of hill and forest and high blue heaven. A sigh went out of him. They had won—well, a small victory. The time vault had been saved from the barbarians. But they were still prisoners and the Lann were still unbeaten.

His head lifted. So were the Dalesmen, he thought defiantly. And by all the gods, so was he himself!

The thundercloud of anger that was half fear died in Lenard's face. Presently he was smiling, and when Kuthay began to mutter about bad luck that would pursue them, he laughed aloud and slapped the old Doctor on the back.

"Why, if the powers in the vault were so mighty and wrathful as you say, the fact that we all escaped unhurt proves that we are the luckiest men alive," he said, and fell to joking with his men until they too grinned and relaxed.

"After all," said Lenard, "the magic would have been helpful, but it's not as if we really needed it. The good swords of Lann are enough."

He rode forward again until he was at Carl's side. "You needn't fear for your lives right away if you behave yourselves," he told the boys. "We're going to rejoin our main army—it's sweeping around the western borders now, and will soon be at Dalestown if it isn't there already. My father and I will keep you for hostages, as you tried to keep me. I daresay that will weaken your father's will to fight, Carl, and so save many lives on both sides."

"Not a very cheering thought for me," answered Carl sourly.

Lenard grew sober. "I wish you wouldn't think of us as devils," he said. "We're a rough crew, yes, and after a long, hard journey through hills and forests to get here, we're entitled to some looting. But few of us are doing this for pleasure or even for power."

"Why, then?" snapped Owl. "For your health, maybe?"

"In a way," replied Lenard. "We're driven to it. Our homeland can't feed us any longer. We must have new lands, and soon."

"I've heard that story before," sneered Tom.

"But you haven't seen it!" cried Lenard. "You haven't watched your thin bitter harvest ruined by hail and rain. You haven't heard babies crying with hunger, and seen your people hollow-eyed from it, and felt it tearing in your own belly. You haven't huddled in a miserable, overcrowded shack while a blizzard howls around you and kills the last few animals you own. You haven't battled the raids of savages from still farther north, driven by their own famine, coming with fire and death and pillage to steal the little remaining to you." His fist raised. "And you haven't seen the sleek, fur-clad trader from the southern tribes pass you by because you've nothing to barter for his meat and grain!"

"We have our own homes," said Carl. "You're just doing to us what has been done to you."

"Of course," answered Lenard. "Because we're a strong folk, a breed of warriors, and aren't meekly going to let our families die if we can take them to a better place. It's nature, Carl. We are the wild dogs killing a stag—because they must if they are to live. But we aren't monsters."

"What would you have the Dalesmen do?" challenged Carl.

"That's up to them," said Lenard, "but if Ralph had any sense, he'd gather his army, which is still pretty good, and retreat with all his people to attack some other, weaker tribe and win new lands."

"And so evil breeds evil, until every man is at his brother's throat. No!"

"As you will." Lenard shrugged. "It was only a thought—

because I wish the Dalesmen no harm, and even admire them in a way. I think you especially, Carl, have the makings of a great Chief, and that you and I together could someday do mighty things, and that it is a shame you are to die in a hopeless fight. But you must make the choice yourself. Think it over.''

He rode off, and Carl sat in silence. The words of the Lann prince seemed to echo in his mind. He couldn't shake free of them. Looking around at the faces of his captors, he saw that they were hardened by war and suffering—but they could smile as a rough joke passed among them. They had wives and children who waited with tears for their home-coming, and if they were wilder than the Dalesmen, it was because their stern land had made them so.

Evil breeds evil—yes, but the great root of today's misery was that man as a whole could not provide himself with a decent living. He had once had the means, in that dim and glorious past which now shone only as a legend and a dream in winter nights—but the means were lost. No, they still existed. The key to that vanished greatness lay in the time vault—but it was taboo.

Suddenly Carl wondered if it had not been a mistake to frighten the Lann from the vault. If they had remained there, and eventually won the war—it would have been a cruel blow for the Dalesmen, but the vault would have been in the hands of a people who were not afraid to use it. In time they might have learned other things, the peaceful arts of the old civilization, and from them it would have spread to all mankind. Many centuries would have been needed, but it might have been the only way to save what was locked in that dark chamber.

What was right? A man should live justly—but too often it was hard to say which was the road of justice. At any rate, this war was not a struggle of evil against good, black against white; it was a fight between many human beings, none of whom was wholly bad or wholly good. If the Dalesmen should somehow win, it would mean slow hunger-death not only for the warriors of Lann but for their innocent women and children in the northlands. What could one do?

He thrust the whirl of confusion out of his mind. It was not, just now, a question of what *should* be done, but of what *could* be done. And the first problem was escape!

At evening the Lann pitched camp in a meadow on the top of a hill. Forest lay on every side, quiet in the gentle sunset light, and it was as if no man had been here since the beginning of the world. The men's preparations were simple, a small fire built to cook the deer which a ranging hunter had brought back, the horses tethered a little way off to graze, blanket rolls spread on the ground for sleeping. Lenard assigned guard duty to three men who would watch in succession, timing themselves as usual by the stars. After supper, the Lann prince came over to the boys with some lengths of rawhide.

"Sorry," he said, "but I'll have to tie you up at night."

"Oh, it's quite all right," said Owl sarcastically. "We just love being tied up."

"It need only be loose, like hobbling a horse," said Lenard. "And you can have some saddle blankets for sleeping."

Carl submitted quietly to the binding. His wrists were lashed together in front of him and a two-foot cord was tied between his ankles, in a sort of harness passing over his shoulders and knotted at the back so that he couldn't reach the knot with his bound hands. It was simple but effective. Tom and Owl were secured in like manner, and Lenard spread some blankets out for them. "Watch these fellows so they don't go releasing each other," he laughed to the guard. "They're lively young scamps."

Darkness stole over the world, stars blinked out and the fire burned to embers. The guard stayed on his feet, pacing up and down, now and then yawning or leaning on his spear. His comrades rolled themselves up and slept with an animal weariness. The horses dozed, or cropped in a night which began to sing with its many noises of cricket and owl and wildcat and startled, running feet.

Carl, Tom and Owl lay with their heads together. From time to time the sentry glanced sharply over at them, but did not try to stop their whispering. The thin new moon rose slowly over the treetops.

"Anything we can do?" breathed Tom. "Any chance to get away?"

"Nah—let's sleep." Owl yawned enormously. "What a day!"

"I wonder—" Carl lay still for so long that his friends thought he had drowsed off himself. But he was thinking.

A stone dug into his right shoulder blade. Lenard should have paid more attention where he spread the blankets. Small matter. Was there any chance of getting away? If there was, did he dare to take it? An attempt which failed would certainly annoy the Lann, perhaps enough so that they'd kill their prisoners.

But that was an unworthy thought, he told himself sharply. His own death was a little thing in this huge world, however much it meant to him. He was son of the Chief and had to live up to the fact.

But how to escape? The Lann slept not far off, the sentry stood armed and alert, and he was trussed up like a pig for slaughter. . . . Curse that stone! His shoulder would be black and blue in the morning.

The idea came all at once. A thin and desperate plan, but— Go ahead! Do it now, at once, before its hopelessness chilled the limbs with fear.

He turned his head. "Tom, are you awake?"

"Yes. What is it?"

"Be ready for things to happen. . . . Owl. Owl, wake up."

"Ugh—uh—whoof! Whazzamatter?"

"Not so loud. Hold yourself ready. I'm going to try something."

Carl waited until the sentry's back was turned. Then he threw off his upper blanket, rose to his knees, and began digging in the ground.

The Lann guard swung about and strode over to him. His spearhead gleamed near the boy's ribs. "What are you doing?" he hissed.

"There's a rock under my back. I'm getting rid of it. See?" Carl pointed to the shadowy form of the stone, where he had pulled aside the lower blanket.

"All right, all right. Don't wake the camp. I'll dig it out for you." The Lann probed in the earth with his spearhead. Carl got to his feet, looking at the stooped back and the helmeted head, thinking with a vague regret, under the thudding of his heart, that the warrior wasn't a bad sort.

There was a chink and the stone rolled free. "There you are," said the man.

"Thanks." Carl stooped over, picking the rock up in one hand. It jutted from his fist, hard and cold and damp with the clinging earth.

Lightning swift, the boy's arms straightened, and his hand crashed the stone against the warrior's temple. The blow shocked back into his muscles, and he heard the dull *crack* as if it were a thunderclap.

The man toppled, blood spurting from his face. Tom was already erect, catching the unconscious body as it fell and easing it to the ground. Owl seized the spear before it could fall clattering. Carl glared wildly at the dim black shapes of the Lann. Someone stirred, mumbling in his sleep.

Bending over, he jerked out the warrior's knife and slashed his bonds across. He handed Tom the weapon to release himself and Owl, while his own fingers groped over the fallen enemy. Blood was hot and sticky as he fumbled with the helmet's chin strap. He got it loose, pulled off the man's dark cloak, and handed both to Tom.

"You're about his height," he hissed. "Wear these and take his spear. Pace up and down, in case someone sees . . ."

They were barely in time. As Tom moved slowly from the boys, a drowsy voice called out: "Whuzzat?"

"It's all well. Go back to sleep," said Tom hoarsely, praying that his tones were not too different from the guard's. He began his slow walk, up and down, up and down. The spear shook in his sweat-slippery hands, and he bit his teeth together to keep them from chattering.

Catlike, snakelike, Carl and Owl were writhing a way through tall grass to the horses. They had the sentry's knife and sword to cut the tether. But if a horse whinnied, or if the unconscious man woke up—Up and down, up and down, pace, pace, pace.

A faint, starlit flash of metal flitted among the animals. Carl and Owl were cutting all the tethers. A horse neighed once, and Tom froze. Then he began pacing again, a guardian figure in cloak and helmet, spear tall against the stars. An enemy, waking briefly, might well suppose that the sentry was still there and that the animal's noise was of no meaning. He might!

The low trilling of a thrush came from the forest's edge. But thrushes rarely sing at night. It was a signal. Tom stared at the camp for a moment. Nothing stirred. He heard a snore and someone talking in his sleep. Turning, he went with long, quiet steps over to the horses.

His friends were holding three by swiftly looped hackamore bridles. The others stirred and snorted, uneasy at this strange doing. Tom laid down his spear and leaped onto the back of one. Carl and Owl followed suit.

A sudden voice thundered from the camp: "Joey! Joey, where are you? What's going on?"

"All right, boys!" Carl's voice lifted high and clear. "Let's go!" He plunged into the thick of the herd, screeching and howling. "Eeeeyah! Hi, hi, hi! Giddap!"

"They're getting away—"

The horses stampeded. Neighing, plunging, they scattered in terror and a wild drumming of hoofs.

"Come on!" barked Carl. "Let's ride to Dalestown!"

An arrow whizzed by his cheek, and another and another. The Lann were awake now, shouting, running about after their mounts, firing at the three who galloped into the forest.

Carl leaned low over the neck of his steed. There hadn't been time to steal spare animals. The risk had been enormous as it was—and so these would flag in a long chase. And a long chase it would be, clear to Dalestown, with the Lann in hot and angry pursuit as soon as they had recovered their own horses.

Owl's laughter pealed forth. "We seem to do nothing but steal livestock these days!" he cried.

"Ride, you ninny!" shouted Carl. "Ride to Dalestown!"

CHAPTER 13

Hero's Reward

THE horse stumbled. Its breath came short and gasping, and foam streaked its dusty flanks. Relentlessly, Carl spurred it with a sharp-pointed twig. The dust cloud behind was growing terribly near.

Weariness blurred the boy's eyes. His head felt empty from lack of rest. There had been no chance to drink all this day, and his mouth was dry. The sun danced cruelly bright above him.

A night and a day, another night and now this day, fleeing, fleeing . . . only the shortest snatches of sleep, more to save the horses than themselves . . . no food, until hunger was a numb ache within them . . . dodging, weaving, splashing along streams, using every trick they knew to hide their trail from the hunters. Now they were on the last stretch, plunging along the well-remembered road to Dalestown, and the riders of Lann were just behind them.

Carl cast a glance to the rear. He could see the forms of men and horses, the up and down of lances and helmets, wavering in heat-shimmer and swirling dust. Since getting on the track of the boys and spotting them about dawn, Lenard and his men had steadily closed the gap between. Their recovered horses, being more in number than the masters and thus able to rest from bearing weight, were fresher. Carl wondered bleakly if his own mount might not fall dead under him.

It might have been wiser to go on foot. A man could run down a horse on any really long stretch. But no, the horse had greater speed for the shorter jogs—such as this last wild lap to Dalestown. No time to think. Too late to think. Ride, ride, ride!

Beside him, Tom and Owl held to the hoof-thudding road, sagging a little with their own exhaustion. Their clothes were ragged, torn by branches in the woods. Their skins were scratched. They were muddy with grime and sweat, weaponless save for one stolen knife, hunted, but they plunged ahead, over the hard-baked dirt of the road, over the hills that rolled to Dalestown.

"Hi-ya!" The savage, wolfish baying of the Lann rang faintly in Carl's ears. An arrow dropped almost beside him, its force spent. But soon the enemy would be well within bowshot-range, and that would be the end.

The land lay broad and green about him, houses growing thicker as he neared the town, grain waving in fields and flowers blooming in gardens. But nothing lived there, nothing stirred, emptiness lay on the world. The people had retreated behind the walls of Dalestown.

The long, easy rhythm of gallop under Carl was breaking as the horse staggered. The Lann howled and spurred their own mounts, closer, closer, a drumbeat roll of hoofs under the brazen heavens.

"Carl—Carl—" Tom's voice was a moan. "We can't make it—so near, but we can't—"

"We can!" shouted the Chief's son, half deliriously. His head rang and buzzed and whirled. He dug fingers into the horse's mane and leaned over the neck. "We're almost there. Hang on, hang on!"

They were speeding up a long slope. As they neared the heights, Carl saw that thunderheads were piling up above it. There would be rain before nightfall and the earth would rejoice. But he—would he be there to feel its coolness?

"Yah, yah, yah!" The Lann yelped and plunged ahead as their prey disappeared over the hilltop.

Dalestown lay below, a dark spot in the green, deep valley, huddled under clouds lifting mountainous overhead. A fresh east wind was springing up, stiffening, whistling eerily in the long grasses and the suddenly tossing trees.

Down the other slope, down toward the walls, gallop, gallop, gallop! Carl risked another glance behind. He could see Lenard's face now in the van of the enemy. The barbarian was smiling.

Blackness grew bright with lightning streaks in the heart of the thunderheads. Clouds were boiling over the sky, flying gray tatters of storm, and the wind's keening rose yet louder. The storm was coming with giant strides.

"We can't make it, Carl." This time it was Owl who gasped out his despair. The wind flung the words raggedly from his mouth. "We just can't make it—"

"We can try!" shouted Carl.

Down and down and down. An arrow sang past, and another and another. Tom's horse neighed shrilly and somehow lengthened its pace. A shaft had grazed its flank.

"Hi, there!" Lenard cupped his hands to yell above the wind and the roaring of trees and the growing boom of thunder. The voice drifted faint to Carl's ears. "Surrender now or we'll shoot you down!"

So near, so near. . . . The valley sides were leveling off now. The massive log walls of Dalestown, the square towers, the high roofs beyond . . . two miles away, perhaps, and every flying step brought them closer . . . but there was no hope. The Lann were yards behind and . . .

Sunlight speared through the clouds, a weird, hard brass-yellow. Thunder banged from heaven to earth and back, shivering the ground. A terrified flock of crows fought the harrying wind as they neared a sheltering thicket.

Carl's muscles tensed for the shaft that would enter his back. He set his teeth against it. He would not cry out even when it tore his lungs . . . but ride, ride, ride!

Laughter snarled almost in his ear. Turning his head, Carl saw the warrior who drew alongside him, thrusting his horse between Tom and the Chief's son. Teeth gleamed in the dark bearded face as a hand reached out for the bridle on Carl's horse.

The boy growled, almost sobbing, and leaned over. With one hand he clung to his steed's mane; the other fingers closed on the braids that hung below the warrior's helmet. He heaved back, reining in his horse as he did. The Lann mount still plunged ahead, and the warrior went crashing from the saddle, one foot caught in a stirrup, howling as he was dragged. Tom snatched the falling lance from the air and whirled about to meet the enemy.

Lightning glared overhead and the rain came, the heavens opening in a gray flood. Stinging silver spears slanted on a whooping wind, splashing back from the earth, hiding the farther hills in a sudden smoke.

Owl had also reined in. A triumphant Lann rider came at him with lifted sword. But Owl still had the knife. He grabbed the raised arm with one hand and slashed it with the other. The warrior yelled, clutching at his blood-spurting wrist, and Owl jerked the sword away and tossed it to Carl.

The Lann closed in on every side, edged metal lifted against the unarmored, rain-streaming bodies. Lightning flamed white in the sky and thunder was a giant war wagon, booming and banging and crashing. Carl lifted his face to the rain, drinking life in a last joyous draught, suddenly unafraid now when hope was gone.

"Take them alive if you can," barked Lenard.

Horses thrusting in, a sudden press of bodies, clubbing lance butts and the flat of swords. . . . Carl swung at the nearest threatening arm, felt his steel bite deep, and then a swung shaft crashed against his head. Lightning and darkness. . . . He toppled from his seat and the rain boiled about him.

Looking dizzily up from where he lay, he saw a horseman seeming to tower above him, lance head pointed against his throat. With a snarl, the boy grabbed the shaft, pushing it aside. His free hand picked up the sword out of the mud, and he hacked out.

He'd not be taken as a hostage and a slave, he thought wildly. He'd make them kill him!

Thunder bawled over the rushing rain and the hooting wind. Carl felt the earth tremble under his feet. Two of the Lann had jumped to the ground and were closing in on him, trying to hem him between their shields. He smote at a helmet and his blade clanged off.

Baroom, baroom, baroom, baroom—Not the thunder shaking the ground, but nearer—sweeping nearer—

The horseman burst out of the storm. His mount was a tall black stallion, and he himself was big and golden-haired and wrathful. Save for shield and helmet, he had no armor, but a broadsword flashed in his hand. He rode full tilt against the group of men.

The great sword yelled out, its rain-wet steel suddenly red, and a warrior died. Another had no time to lift blade before he too was cut down. The plunging horse was reined in, rearing back on its hind legs, and the pawing hoofs smashed against a third barbarian. Steel clamored against steel as the newcomer hewed at a fourth man. A fifth rode against his left side, sword aloft. Raging like a tiger, the golden-haired man straightened his left arm, and the spiked boss on his shield crashed into the face of the northerner.

"Father!" yelled Carl. "Father!"

Ralph's smile was savage in his beard. He knocked the sword spinning from his enemy's hand and the man had barely time to skitter aside before that screaming blade scythed him down. And now other forms were coming from Dalestown. Carl saw Ezzef and three more guards in the lead, saw lances lowered and heard the faint scream of a horn.

The Lann, suddenly outnumbered, whirled their steeds about and went galloping back whence they came. Roaring vengefully, the Dalesmen swept after them, until Ralph winded his horn. Then, slowly and grudgingly, they straggled back to their Chief.

Ralph had already sprung from the saddle to fold Carl in his arms. "I saw you from afar," he choked. "I saw them after you, and came as fast as I could. Are you well? You're hurt."

"A scratch." Carl hugged his father. "Tom? Owl?"

"Still alive," said the younger boy. The pounding rain had plastered his sandy hair flat, and the blood running from his cut scalp was dissolved before it had trickled to his breast. He grinned weakly.

Ezzef came riding up, his horse splashing mud, his face darkened. "We could've had 'em, if you hadn't called us back," he complained.

"It might have led you into a trap," said Ralph. "The Lann, the main army, are very close." He straightened. "Come on, let's get back into town."

Mounted again, Carl rode slowly with his father. The Chief's face was grave. "You went to the City, didn't you?" he said.

"Yes," answered Carl.

Ralph shook his head. "That was not wise. Donn is determined to enforce the law. You'll hardly be able to lie out of his accusation, and—well—"

"It was for the good of the tribe," said Carl heavily.

"Of course. But the tribe may not see it that way." Ralph clapped his son's shoulder, "However, I'll do what I can. I didn't rescue my only son from his enemies to see him hanged by his friends."

The gates yawned before them. As they entered, Carl saw that the streets were jammed with people. As far as he could see, the crowd surged in the rain, drenched and miserable and hungry-looking.

Tents and lean-tos were thrown up everywhere, in courtyards and streets and market places, a swarming city within a city. By order of the Chief and the Council, every home and warehouse and shop, any building that could hold a person, was filled with the overflow of refugees. All food had gone into a common store, and the town gave a grudging ration out of the kitchens it had taken over. Already, even before the Lann were in sight, Dalestown was under siege.

The people were packed together, townsfolk and country dwellers and the hunters and charcoal burners and lumbermen of remote forests. Women held babies in their arms, shielding them against the rain, and other children clung to their skirts. Men were armed, grim and angry of face. Old folk looked around, timid and bewildered, a lifetime had toppled to ruin about them. The crowd moved aimlessly, hopelessly, buzzing and mumbling under the steady roll of thunder. Eyes, eyes, a thousand eyes stared at the returning warriors.

"Has all the tribe come here?" whispered Carl.

"No," said Ralph bleakly. "Only those who could make it. But that's more than we can really hold. Keeping order in that mob is more than enough for our guards to do, besides manning the lookout posts—and the food isn't going to last very long. And, if they're crowded together like this for several weeks, there'll be sickness. Oh, it's bad, it's very bad."

Lightning blazed luridly in the windy heavens. A group of solemn Doctors approached the Chief. Two of them bore holy symbols aloft. Two were beating drums. Two chanted spells against witchcraft. In their lead, tall and old and grim, stalked Donn.

His robes clung to him in the lashing rain, his face was streaming with the chill watery flow, but there was no weakness and no mercy in the eagle face that lifted up to Carl. His voice came harsh and clear through the storm: "You have been to the City."

Carl forced himself to meet those terrible eyes. "I have," he said. It would be worse than useless to deny what was plain to everyone.

"You knew it was forbidden. You knew death is the penalty."

"And I knew it was our only chance to save ourselves!" Carl turned to the ranked people where they stood in the rain, staring and waiting. "I know there is wisdom in the City, not witchcraft, not devils or Doom, but wisdom, craft and knowledge to drive off the

Lann and rebuild the ancient glories of man. My friends and I risked our lives to go there for the sake of the tribe. For your sakes, O people.''

"And you brought down the anger of the gods!" cried Donn. He pointed at the boys, but it was to the Dalesmen that he shouted. "They went to the City once and entered the taboo circle and brought back a piece of the cursed magic. Our army was beaten at the battle of the river. They went again and dealt with the witches and fiends. The Lann are at our gates and our homes lie waste. People of the Dales, the gods have turned their faces from you. The wrath of the gods lies heavy on us, and we have been given into the hands of our enemies!"

"Aye—aye—aye—" The voices rumbled, sullen, hating, the voices of a folk frightened and desperate and looking for a scapegoat. There had been nothing but bad luck. Something must have angered the gods, and the High Doctor was the man who knew their dark will. Fists were shaken and swords began to gleam.

"The blasphemers must die!"

"Yes, yes, yes—Hang them, hang them now—" It was like a chorus of wolves baying. The mob pressed closer, the fierce blink of lightning gleamed on eyes and bared teeth.

"No!" Ralph's roar was like the thunder come to earth. His sword flamed suddenly free, and his loyal guards drew their own blades and formed a ring about the boys.

"If they have done a crime," shouted Ralph, "let them be tried as is the right of all Dalesmen. Are you beasts that would kill on one man's word? I swore to uphold the law of the Dales, and I'll do it at sword's point if I must!"

"Then let them be thrown in prison," shrilled Donn. "Let the Council judge them tomorrow."

Ralph's sword lowered as the crowd fell away. "So be it," he said wearily. "Let them be jailed, as the law demands." He touched his son's cheek, briefly and tenderly. "I'm sorry, Carl."

The boy tried to smile. "It's all right, Father."

Ezzef led a squad of guards to take the three friends to jail. The young guardsman was outraged. "If that's the law," he cried, "then it's a duty to break it!" He lowered his voice. "If you fellows want to make a dash for freedom, I don't think any of us could, uh, grab you in time."

"A dash to the Lann? No, thanks!" Carl grimaced. "Anyway, I

want a chance to plead my case before the Council. I'm going to try and get that stupid taboo lifted.''

"I'll spread the word," said Ezzef. "There've been rumors about your last expedition to the City. A lot of us younger men think you're probably right. At least, that you ought to get a fair hearing. We'll all be at the meeting tomorrow." His face darkened. "And if everything goes against you, if you really are sentenced to swing, we'll see what can be done about rescuing you. Nor do I think your father is so inhumanly upright that he wouldn't give us a hand in that case!"

"We'll see." Carl's voice was flat with weariness. "Right now I just want to sleep."

The jail was a small, solid building near the great market square. It was watched over by a middle-aged guard and his wife, who were themselves indignant at seeing three boys facing death after having fought for the tribe that threatened them now. They prepared baths and supper, and locked the prisoners into a small clean cell of their own. The other rooms were crowded with men serving short terms for the brawling that was unavoidable in the over-full town.

When the door closed behind him, Owl yawned and stretched and broke into a chuckle. "First the witches jug us, then the Dalesmen," he said. "And in between, we were held by the Lann. I guess we just aren't popular."

"Who cares?" Tom's voice was blurred with sleep, and he stumbled almost blindly for one of the straw ticks on the floor.

Carl stood for a moment looking out of the small, iron-barred window. The rain was still falling heavily, the street was running with water and muck, the town lay dark beyond. Yes, he thought wearily, yes, his was a strange destiny. He seemed to be an outcast everywhere in the world because he bore a mystery in his heart.

Well—tomorrow—He slept.

That night the Lann army marched its last lap. Dalesmen saw burning houses red against the horizon and heard the tramping of thousands of feet and hoofs, the clinking of metal and the guttural voices of men. When the dawn mists lifted, they saw a ring of steel about their walls, campfires burning, horses staked out in grain-fields, and the savage myriads of Lann prowling around the defense.

The last stronghold was besieged.

CHAPTER 14

Council in Dalestown

UNDER the law of the Dales, every tribesman was a member of the Council and could attend its meetings on summons of the Chief if he chose, to help make new laws and reach important decisions. The Council was also the highest court, though ordinary trials were given over to a jury of elders. But this was to be no common proceeding, and the criers and drums of the meeting had been calling since dawn.

Some warriors had to stand guard in the towers and watch the encircling Lann, and as always, there were men who would not trouble themselves to attend a Council even when they were able. But rumor had been flying throughout the night and the morning. By noon the Hall was full.

Ralph mounted the stage at its northern end with a slow, grave step. He was clad in black, with a white mantle hanging from his shoulders and the golden-hilted sword of justice at his side. After him came Donn, leaning on the arm of a young Doctor, and then the elders of the tribe. They took their seats and waited.

Carl and his friends were led by an armored guard onto the stage and found chairs there. The buzz of voices grew almost to a roar. For a moment Carl was afraid. He saw the hundreds upon hundreds of eyes all staring at him, and it was worse than the spears of the Lann. Then a single deep voice shouted above the noise—''Give it to 'em, lads! You've done well!'' Courage returned and he sat down, folding his arms and looking stiffly ahead.

He knew the Hall from many past times, but he studied it now as if he were a stranger. The great building was one huge room; its rafters high, high above the men who surged and chattered below. From those rafters hung the ancient banners of the Dalesmen—that ragged flag had been carried by Valthor the Victorious, that dusty standard had lifted over the stricken field of Seven Rivers. The glories of the past stirred and rustled in their dreams. The walls were paneled in carved wood, gods and heroes and animals caught in a rich glow of polished oak. The wooden pillars that marched down the length of the Hall on either side were graven with leaves and fruits from the Tree of Life. Tapestries of the finest weave draped the windows, through which sunlight and air came streaming to the shadowy cavern of the chamber. From the stage to the door, the Hall was filled with benches, and now they were packed and crowded with men, the overflow standing in the aisles and beyond the entrance. Each man was armed, since there might be an alarm at any moment, and the sheen of metal was fierce in that hot, restless half-light.

Sweeping his eyes over the Hall, Carl saw that he was not without supporters. John the farmer sat strickenly in the front row. Near by was a solid bloc of young men who had apparently come in a body; Ezzef waved at Carl from that section. And there were others, old family friends, comrades of game and chase, whose looks were sympathetic.

The boy tried to relax. He was bathed, fed and rested. His wounds were bandaged, and Ralph had sent clean garments for him and his companions. He could do nothing just now. But excitement thrummed high in him; he strained and quivered with it. This was more than his own life. Perhaps the future of the world would be settled today.

A gong boomed, once, twice, thrice. Slowly the talk died away and was replaced by a breathless, waiting silence.

Ralph and Donn went through the old ritual of opening a Council. They avoided each other's eyes. Then the Chief stepped forth. His tones rang deep and clear.

"I am supposed to preside over this, as all meetings," he said. "But a judge may not take sides, and I think you all know that my own feelings are too deeply caught here. Therefore, I shall turn the

Council over to Wellan, chief of the elders, and speak only as a tribesman.'' He unbuckled the sword of justice and handed it gravely to the white-headed old man seated at his right.

Owl hissed furiously, ''He's betraying us! As Chief, he could at least swing things to save our lives. He's too law-abiding!''

''No, you fool,'' muttered Tom. ''This way is better. As Chief he could not even try to change whatever is going to happen, or people would know and howl him down. Under the law, he has no power to do more than preside. But as a tribesman, he can speak freely—and people will still know he's the real Chief and listen more closely to him than to others.'' He smiled. ''Carl, your father may be upright, but he's not stupid either!''

''We are met to try three for breaking taboo,'' came old Wellan's reedy voice. ''I am told that this is also a meeting to decide if the taboo is not to be lifted. Let the accuser speak.''

Donn rose to his feet and walked to the front of the stage. His eyes smoldered over the Council, and when he spoke it was slowly and sorrowfully.

''This is a heavy thing for me,'' he began. ''I must turn on a family whose members have been my lifelong friends and helpers. I must call for the death of three promising youths who sought only to aid their tribe in this terrible war. The hand of the gods lies grimly on me.

''But a Doctor's path is stern. He is sworn to forget not only himself, but all others, in serving the gods and the tribe. I have myself, in my younger days, closed my ears to the screaming of poor children from whom I pulled an infected tooth or cut a devouring growth. Yet afterward they lived because of what I had done, and thanked me for it. Now I must again hurt that I may heal. But this time the sickness is deeper. It is a sickness of the spirit, and the wrath of heaven lies on us because of it.''

He went on to describe the first visit of the boys and the trophy they had brought back—and how he had destroyed the thing with many purifying rites and hoped that the curse had been taken off. But apparently it had not, for the brave and wisely led army of the Dales had been routed by a smaller force of enemies—enemies who now held the entire land in their grip and had penned the tribe in its walls like cattle in a corral. Yet some devil must still have lurked in these boys, for they had stolen away again to the forbidden City, and had dealt with the witch-folk, and returned to preach openly the breaking of taboo. And what ruin might not come of that second insolence toward heaven? The gods might visit all the folk with plague; or they might let them die in here of slow hunger; or they might aid the Lann to break through and butcher the people and set the town ablaze.

No, the tribe had to disown these mad boys who had thus broken the laws of the wise ancients. It had to appease heaven with the greatest sacrifice of all: human life taken according to law. "And thereafter," finished Donn, "the gods may take pity on us and grant us the victory. But I will weep alone in darkness."

He turned slowly back to his chair and sat down again. His hands trembled. The Hall buzzed and mumbled until Wellan had the gong sounded again. Then the old man called, "Let the accused speak."

Carl got up. "We have decided that I will speak for all three of us," he said, striving for quietness and dignity. He put his hands on his hips and stood looking over the assembly for a moment.

"I am not one to argue logic and religion with the wise Donn," he went on. "However, I should like to make one or two points now, in answer to the questions just raised.

"First, it is said that we suffered our defeat at the hands of the Lann because of this visit to the City where I obtained the cold light. May I point out that we three were not the first to enter the taboo circle. It had often been done before, even if no one stayed very long. Furthermore, we did so under press of mortal danger, and the law of the Dales permits a man to save his life in any way necessary. Moreover, the first disaster to us, the Lann invasion of the northern marches, the defeat of the gathered men there, and the sack of all that territory, happened *before* we took this light away. So how could it be due to the anger of the gods? Surely they are not so unjust as to punish a deed before it is done—or, for that matter, to visit the sins of three heedless boys on a whole tribe."

He looked at his father. "Sir, you led the army. Do you think our defeat was due to divine anger?"

Ralph stood up. "I do not," he said flatly. "We were beaten because the Lann had a better army. More cavalry, not more virtue. Also, we cut our way out of their trap and escaped with fewer losses than even I had hoped for. Offhand, I should think the gods took pity on us, rather than vengeance." He sat down again.

"As for the second trip to the City," went on Carl, "again, you and your families fleeing here, and the Lann sweeping through the

Dales, happened before the crime which is supposed to have caused them. In short, O Council, I think common sense shows that whether or not anyone goes to the City has nothing to do with whether or not we win our battles. Except in this way: that by the power of the ancients which is hidden away there, we can find our victory! Let me now tell you the full story of these two visits and you shall judge for yourselves whether we did right or not.''

He gave them the tale, speaking in the plain words that he knew these earthy farmers and workmen liked. He dwelt on the great good spirit which had created the time vault in the hope that men would find it and use it well, and he told them a few things the ancients had undoubtedly been able to do. He finished simply: ''Thus I ask the Council, which makes all laws, to raise the taboo on the old works. It was born of fear and ignorance; let us be bold and wise. Let us send our army forth from these walls, to drive through the Lann ring and capture that vault. Let us learn from it—first, some simple way to defeat our present foes—then, how to rebuild that glorious lost world. That is all.''

He sat down, and the assembly chamber muttered and seethed with voices. Men stirred restlessly, talking to their neighbors, turning this new thought over in slow minds. Someone stood up and screamed for the instant death of the blasphemers, but was shut up by an armed guard. The tone that grew slowly out of the noise was confused: many were frightened and hostile and wanted a hanging, many were simply bewildered, a few cried for the release of the prisoners and the changing of the law.

Donn stood up again. ''This is heresy!'' he shouted. ''Men only make the laws of men. They cannot change the laws of the gods.''

Carl could not suppress a grin, even then with the shadow of the noose on him. Hardly a Dalesman had any idea of what ''heresy'' could be; the gods were mysterious powers to which one sacrificed and made magic, that was all. Donn had spent so many years in his few old books that he had lost the feeling of life.

But others were more dangerous. Taboo was a very real and terrible thing, whose breaking was sure to cause ruin. They yelled for the boys' deaths. But magic could be set against magic; a man armed with the sorceries of the ancients could laugh at the powers of the gods. So there were others who shook their weapons and cried they would burn the gallows first.

Ezzef's voice lifted over the gathering roar: ''Who stands

with us? Who'll fight to save these lads and conquer the City?''

"I, I, I!" Swords leaped out. The group of young men stood up and waved their blades whistling in the air. Others, scattered through the Hall, pushed toward them.

"Kill the luckless ones!" A giant farmer rose, brandishing his ax. "Kill them and appease the gods!"

"No!" John was on his feet now. "No, I'll fight for them—"

"Order!" wailed the elder feebly. "Order! Remember the law!"

The gong thundered. Its brazen voice was almost lost in the rising clamor. Swords were aloft and men scrambled for a place to fight.

Ralph sprang to the front of he stage. His great voice bellowed forth like angry thunder: "Stop! Stop this! Sit down! I'll kill the first peacebreaker myself!"

That turned their heads. They saw him towering there, stern and wrathful, a spear poised in one hand. They knew he could fling it to the farther end of the Hall and slay. They knew he was the Chief.

Slowly, grumbling and growling, the men lowered their weapons and sat down. Slowly the storm died. When it was past and the silence lay heavy, Ralph's scorn was whiplike:

"Are you the Dalesmen, or are you wild dogs? What madness is this? With the enemy at our very walls, haven't you got enough fighting to do? Or do you want to play into their hands and make them a present of all we've striven for? Hah, I don't know why I should bother leading you. I'd sooner lead a pack of woods-runners. Now be quiet and listen!"

All had forgotten that he was not presiding, that he spoke only as a common tribesman. "We have to work together," he said, his tones now earnest and persuasive. "We have to forget grudges and differences until this common danger is past. Let us therefore reach a decision quickly, and let it be by the old method of law. Will all who favor keeping the taboo and hanging the boys raise their hands?"

There were many hands that went up, thought Carl sickly. Some rose at once, some came slowly and hesitatingly, but the majority voted for death.

Ralph did not stir a muscle, and his speech was unwavering. "Now let those who wish to change the law and release the boys raise their hands." Perhaps a hundred were lifted, mostly by younger men.

"Very well." Ralph smiled. Only those on the stage were close enough to see the sweat that beaded his forehead. "As is the custom of the Dales, I suggest we compromise. Since most of us want to keep the law as it is, let it be so. But to satisfy the other party, let us set these lads free on their promise not to violate the taboo again. And if the gods grant us victory, we shall give them a double sacrifice at the next festival."

That drew nods and muttered agreement from the bulk of the people. A few men, as usual, had to make speeches proposing this or that, or simply for or against Ralph's suggestion, but it didn't take long. In the end, the Council voted to adopt the motion, and Wellan closed the meeting.

The great assembly filed out slowly, talking and arguing. John sprang up on the stage and folded his sons in his arms, weeping without shame. Ralph wiped his face and grinned at Carl.

"Whew!" he said. "That was close!"

"Too close," said Carl. He felt no relief. There was a bitter taste in his mouth.

Donn shook his head. "I do not know if this was wise," he said. "But—" Suddenly he smiled. "But believe me, Carl, I'm glad. If misfortune is to come, then let it!" His eyes grew piercing. "Now come with me to the temple and take the oath."

Carl stiffened his back. "No," he said.

"What?" screeched Donn.

"I will not promise. Instead, I swear I will go back to the City whenever I can—again and again—until that vault is open!"

"You're mad!" cried Ralph. "Carl, you're raving!"

"You must die," said Donn in a dead voice.

"No!" Ralph stepped forth. "Can't you see? He's sick. Maybe he's possessed by a devil. I don't know. But he isn't himself."

"That may be." Donn stroked his chin. "Yes, that may well be. The curse of the City can work in strange ways." He came to a decision. "I'll do what I can to drive the devil from him," he said. "Tomorrow I'll come with all that's needful. But meanwhile he must go back to jail."

Ralph bit his lip. After a long while, he nodded.

Carl was led away. No one had noticed that Tom and Owl had left with their father, making no promises either. Or else they had not been thought important enough to matter. Ralph walked from the Hall out into the market square. His face was drawn, and he smote his hands together in pain.

CHAPTER 15

The Friendless Ones

IT'S SHAMEFUL!'' said Ezzef. "It's a cursed, crying shame!'' He sat on a bench outside one of Dalestown's public stables, leaning forward with fists clenched on knees. Tom and Owl had slipped from their joyful parents to meet him and stood before the young guard. Half a dozen others also gathered around, reckless youths who had shouted for blood in the Council and still chafed at its decision. All bore arms and all were angry.

Tom had just reported what had happened to Carl—he'd heard rumors that his friend was back in prison, and had stopped to talk with him through the barred window. "And tomorrow," he finished, "the Doctors will come with their drums and rattles and vile potions, to drive out the fiend they think has possessed him."

"I doubt if there's any such thing," said Owl. "But that kind of treatment will break anybody's will in time."

"I don't know if they'd get an oath from Carl," scowled Ezzef. "He's always been a stubborn sort when he thought he was in the right."

"In that case," said Nicky, a son of Black Dan, "they'll end up hanging him after all."

"By that time," answered Tom gloomily, "the Lann will be here and may do the job for them."

"Yes, so." Ezzef waved a sinewy hand at the nearest watchtower, where it bulked over the thatch and wood roofs. "They're waiting outside—just waiting, curse them! That's all they need to do. Hunger and sickness will fight for them within our walls."

"I suppose Ralph will sally forth against the enemy," said Sam the Strong, who was a blacksmith's apprentice.

"Heh!" Willy Rattlehead's bucktoothed mouth split in a grin. "And be mowed like ripe wheat. Oh, it'll make a fine hero-song, when we're all dead."

"Now wait," said Ezzef. "Let's not get sidetracked. I called you fellows together because I wanted to talk with someone I trusted. Tom, Owl, tell me—how much power is there in that vault? Honestly."

"I don't know much about it," shrugged Tom. "But you heard Carl tell in the meeting about that devil powder which scared the Lann from the City. Some of that, all by itself, could stampede their horses—which'd make a big difference in battle. And then the first time we were there, and old Ronwy was showing us through the vault, he was saying something about a simple flying machine. He called it a balloon, and said it wasn't hard to make. Imagine throwing rocks and boiling water from above!"

"There must be more," added Owl. "Lots more. We're just trying to remember what was there that we could put to quick use. Something called rockets—fire arrows, sort of, but charged with the devil powder—"

"That's enough," Ezzef cut in. "I don't understand it. Don't think you boys do either. Carl does, a little, and this witch-chief seems to know a lot. Nor can the witches stand against even a few good warriors, so a strong band wouldn't have to worry about them. D'you see what I'm getting at?"

Tom's eyes glowed. "Yes!"

"We're not the only ones who'd go on such an expedition," said Ezzef. "I know at least a dozen others that'd jump at the chance. Didn't have time to get word to them of this little meeting, but they're biting the bit right now, I swear."

"So—" Nicky's dark face grew taut. "So we get Carl out of the jug, and sneak from this town and through the enemy lines, and make our way to the City. There we'll have to drive off the witch-patrols. We're taking the wild chance that Carl and this Ronwy can cook up something useful. If that doesn't work, why, we've betrayed our tribe and are outlaws even if they do somehow win.''

"You needn't go if you're afraid," snapped Tom.

"Oh, I'm not afraid," said Nicky evenly. "I'll be glad to go. I just wanted to make sure everybody understood the risks we'd have to run."

"Not much risk," grunted Ezzef. "Because we've really nothing to lose. All right, boys, are you game?"

Night crept westward. Carl's cell darkened before the sky had faded, and he stood at the window looking out to the blue strip of heaven until it had turned black and starry. Then he sighed and lay down on his crude mattress.

It was quiet in here. Ralph had forbidden lights after dark while the siege lasted, lest they start a fire in the overcrowded town, and folk went to bed with the sun. Now there would only be the guards at gate and tower, and the night watch tramping down the streets. The town slept, and about its slumber glowed the ominous red of the Lann campfires, and the sounds of the enemy laughing and singing and sharpening swords drifted in its dreams.

Carl couldn't doze off. He lay bolt awake, turning restlessly, staring open-eyed into the gloom. What was he to do?

He'd hurt his father, who had fought so valiantly in battle and Council to save his life. He'd gotten himself locked away, when he might be of use patrolling the beleaguered town. In the morning he would face a crazed drumming and dancing, and be scourged and given nauseating drinks, to expel the devil they thought was in him. And for what? For a lost cause, for a will-o'-the wisp, for a stubbornness which would not surrender even in defeat.

In the end, he knew, he would give up and take the oath. While he lived there was always hope—someone else might be persuaded to break taboo. But then why did he refuse now? Why did he suffer a useless confinement and visit an unnecessary pain on those who loved him? Was he becoming another Donn, so sternly devoted to the Tribe that he had no time or mercy for the mere tribespeople?

Was he right, even? Who was he to challenge laws made centuries before his birth? Was he so much wiser than his elders that he could tell them what was truth?

Or even if he was right, even if the old powers could again be given to the world—was that for the best? How did he know that the ancients had been happy? How did he know that a rebuilding would not start anew the terrible old cycle of wars and cruelty and woe, until the world crashed in a second Doom?

Carl tried to shake the doubts out of his tormented mind, but they returned to plague him, little formless devils mocking and gibbering in the depths of his brain. He muttered wearily and wondered how late in the night it was.

There came a sudden, scuffling noise outside the door. A voice growled something, metal clinked faintly, feet slid over the packed dirt—Carl leaped from rest, every nerve drawn wire-taut, and strained against the solid bulk of the door.

"Carl!" The whisper drifted through, dim and unrecognizable. "Carl, wake up!"

"I'm here," he gasped. "Who is this?"

"It's Owl. Stand by. We're going to break in."

Carl drew a shuddering breath. "What is this—"

"Not so loud! You'll wake the other prisoners. All right, Sam!"

A hammer rang on iron, muffled by a fold of cloth laid between. Once, twice, thrice, and then the clumsy padlock jingled to ruin and the door creaked open.

The figures of Carl's rescuers were vague shadows in the hall. There were four, armed and armored, peering nervously out the jail entrance into the silent street. Owl stepped forth. He bore equipment in his hands—helmet, breastplate, shield, knife and sword—which he gave into Carl's amazed grasp. "Get this on quick," he muttered.

"But—but—"

"It's a rescue. Don't you see? Twenty of us are here to get you out and follow you to the City. Now fast!"

For a moment longer Carl stood unmoving, and all his doubts rose to overwhelm him. Then decision came and suddenly he was swift and cool, throwing on his clothes, buckling the armor over them, no thought save the tremendous will to freedom.

Yes, one—the gentle old couple who guarded the jail and had looked after him—"What about the guard here and his wife?"

"They're all right. We went into their bedroom, bound and gagged them, that's all. They'll be found in the morning. But we can't rouse the others held in here or they'll make a racket that'll bring the night watch down on us like a star falling. All set? Let's go, then."

They slipped out of the corridor and the entrance, into the street. Houses loomed tall on either hand, shadowing, turning the narrow way into a river of darkness. A cat squalled from a roof, a dog barked answer, a man shouted something angry out of an upper window, the leather of the fugitives squeaked and the metal rang faintly—the night seemed alive with noise, and Carl started at every sound.

He had time for a brief regret. If they were caught trying to escape, it would go harder with his rescuers than with him; if they were caught by the Lann, it would most likely mean death for all; if they reached the City and failed to produce the promised magic, they would forever be marked traitors and outlaws. In any case, it would be still another cruel blow to the many that Ralph and John had endured.

His will grew tight again. This was no age for weaklings. You had to do whatever seemed best, without letting gods or men or the lower devils deter you.

The measured tramping of feet came nearer. They crouched into a narrow alley and watched the town guard go by, armored guards with axes on their shoulders. For a moment, it seemed as if the relentless march would go through their very hiding place, but the guards turned sharply and went on down the street.

Farther along, winding between the tents of refugees, the little band saw two men approaching. At Carl's hurried command, they fell into formation and moved steadily forward. The strangers fled. They must have been out to do a little thieving, and had taken the escaping ones for the watch.

Now softly, softly, glide between walls up to the great stockade, hug its shadow and slip along, slip along . . .

Two ladders seemed to spring out of darkness. Tom and Ezzef stood by them with drawn swords. "There you are," whispered the young guard. "All right, Carl. The rest have gone ahead. We go by twos, up the ladders, jump to the ground outside, and then the gods get us through the enemy camp. Meet at dawn by the swimming hole in old Rogga's woods. After that, you're the leader."

Carl nodded and went softly up the rungs, holding his body close to the ladder. At the top he hesitated, glancing at the watchtowers looming against the sky. It was a cloudy, dark night, but even so the guards would be alert— Nothing to do but jump!

He sprang, relaxing his body and falling twenty feet with trained ease. He landed in one of the hedges clustered below the walls, feeling branches rake him, more concerned with the noise of his armor. But that wasn't much. The crackling twigs were louder, and he lay stiff for a moment, waiting for a challenge.

No answer, no sound. The fortress stood black and massive above him, crouched into itself, waiting for an unknown doom. Owl joined him and the two pairs of eyes turned to the scattered red flicker of enemy fires, half a mile away.

"Let's go," said Carl at last.

He drew his mantle up to cover the sheen of helmet and breast-plate, and loped cautiously toward the besieging camp, weaving from tree to bush to thicket, waiting tense at every sound that drifted from the foe. Discovery meant flashing swords and red death. They had forfeited the help of Dalestown. Truly, thought Carl, his was a friendless gang and every man's hand was against it. Briefly, he wondered if the great pioneers who had built the lost civilization had been as lonely in their day.

Closer, closer. Carl lay prone behind a bush and looked slit-eyed at the ring he had to cross. Some twenty yards off on either side, a dying campfire cast its dull light on sleeping men, stacked weapons, an occasional tent; between was a lane of darkness. Two fires down, several Lann were still sitting up, drinking wine robbed from some Dale house; their bawling songs came vaguely upwind. A cow taken for butchering lowed in the night. Somewhere a horse whinnied.

"Let's go," hissed the boy again.

He wormed a slow way from behind the shrub, through the trampled grass, between the fires. Often he halted, heart a-thunder, so that anyone who had chanced to see a movement would suppose it was wind rippling the grass. He was almost through the barrier when he heard the squeak of boots.

One of the Lann who had been drinking was going back to his own campfire to sleep. He staggered a little. Glancing up, Carl saw a dim red sheen of light on the grinning face. But he lurched away, and Carl's breath whistled out between his clenched teeth.

So far, so good. Now came the hard part.

CHAPTER 16

Defiance of the Gods

FOUR days later, in the middle of morning, Carl looked again on the City. It had been a hard trek on foot which he and his little band had made. They went across country, avoiding the roads which were still used by occasional marauding northerners, but even so they had often had to conceal themselves as a troop of Lann rode by. The countryside had been green and quiet for the most part; houses still stood and the burned, gutted shells Carl had expected were actually few. After all, the barbarians would not ruin too many of the homes they expected to occupy themselves. But Chief Raymon had his men out scouring the Dales to find livestock and stored grain to feed the besieging army.

Now and then Carl's force encountered people of their own tribe. Some had even stayed in their houses, hoping for a miracle before the terrible plunderers should come to them. Most wandered gypsy-like, gleaning what food they could, hiding by day and traveling by night. Many, Carl learned, had retreated into the great forests, taking up a hunter's existence. They were not panicky, but there was a look of misery about them, the look of the defeated and uprooted, which wrenched the boy's heart.

His men had of necessity turned thieves themselves, stealing whatever grain or animals they had been able to find. But otherwise it would have gone to the Lann, and Carl promised himself to repay such of the owners as he could identify later. If he lived!

Now he stood with his men crowding behind him, looking past the wilderness of the outer City to the distantly gleaming towers.

Ezzef's awed whisper came to his ears: "It's—big, isn't it?"

"And so still." Sam the Strong had never quailed before danger he could see and fight, but now he clutched a rabbit's foot tightly. "But it seems to be watching. Are you sure it's safe, Carl?"

"It hasn't killed me yet," snapped the boy.

"What do we do now?" asked Nicky. It was a strange feeling, having these warriors, most of them some years older than the Chief's son, turning to him for guidance—a strange and lonely feeling. Carl was glad that to Tom and Owl he was still only a friend.

"We'll go straight to the witch-folk," he decided. "Might as well have it out with them now. Come on—and be careful."

They went down the streets in a tight square. The early sun blinked off their drawn weapons. Walls closed in on either hand, high and silent. Some of the Dalesmen looked nervously about, feeling that a trap was closing on them.

"It's nothing to fear," said Carl. His voice came oddly flat in that immense quiet. "Just brick and stone and metal and broken glass. Even the machines in the vault are dead until a man uses them."

On and on. The most ruinous sections fell behind. The buildings grew taller, lifting magnificently toward a smiling heaven. Now and then a faint noise would make men start, but it was only a rat or a gopher or a wheeling bird. Until—

The arrow whizzed from above and thunked quivering into Tom's bullhide shield. Carl yelled an order, and the Dalesmen sprang into a tight-bunched knot of warriors, holding their shields in front of them, peering over the tops. Four witch-men leaned out of a gaping third-story window and shot. Somewhere else a horn screamed, and a drum began to thutter.

"Get away—on the double!" shouted Carl.

Arrows sleeted after them as the invaders trotted down the street. The rearward men ran backward, shields aloft to protect the band. Shafts thudded home, caught in the toughened leather, rattling off helmets, now and then grazing a leg or an arm. But these were not from the hundred-pound longbows of the Dales, whose missiles could drive through an iron corselet—the witches pulled a feeble bow, and before long Carl's party was out of range.

Then they faced forward and swung down the resounding way,

hot with anger. The old skyscrapers loomed near, and the frantic drums rolled loud. A woman ran screeching from the warrior's path. A dog yelped on their heels.

They burst into the main section and were confronted by the men of the City. The witches had grabbed weapons and gathered in a harried force. Even now, others were racing from shops and homes and gardens to join their fellows. The Dalesmen reformed their square and looked boldly at the spears slanting toward them. They were outnumbered five or six to one, but they had armor and they were trained and the purpose within them was insuperable.

"Where is Ronwy?" said Carl, speaking to an old man in a splendid cloak who seemed to be the leader. "I want to speak to your Chief."

"Ronwy is not our Chief," answered the witch sullenly. His followers stirred behind him, lips tightened by fear and hate.

It was like a knife stabbing Carl's heart. "Ronwy is—dead?" he gasped.

"He has angered the gods. His witchcraft brought fire and thunder and the devils of Atmik to earth. He cannot be our Chief. We came back after the Lann were gone and imprisoned him."

"Ronwy lives!" Relief left Carl feeling weak.

"I know you," said the witch-leader. "You are the ill-omened one who first came here and brought all this woe on us. I forbid you the City. Go, before we kill all of you."

Carl shook his head. "No," he said. "We have come to free Ronwy and open the time vault. Stop us if you dare."

"We are more than you," blustered the witch-man. "Many, many more. You can kill some of us, perhaps, but in the end we'll cut you down."

"Go ahead, then!" Carl stepped slowly forward, sword raised, glaring from behind his shield. "Who'll be the first to die?"

His followers pressed behind him, locking their shields together, a walking wall which bristled with sharp-edged metal. The disorderly ranks of the witchmen stirred, muttering and backing up before that grim advance.

"This is our home!" The old witch-chief's voice was almost a sob. "You've no right—"

"We don't mean to violate your homes," said Carl. "We won't enter anyone's shop or dwelling. But the time vault is not yours. It belongs to all the world, and we claim it for the world."

"Kill them!" screamed the leader.

Weapons clashed and rattled, but no one stepped from the milling crowd. Carl grinned savagely and went on walking toward his opponents.

"We'll go to the Lann!" babbled the witch-chief. "We'll get them to help us drive you out!"

"All right, boys," said Carl. "Scatter them."

The Dalesmen let out a spine-shivering yell and broke into a crashing, jingling trot. Swords and axes were aloft, pikes slanted forward, arrows fitted to tensed bowstrings. They were only twenty, but at sight of that band, the witches broke. They stumbled away, some running, some slinking and snarling, but none dared to stand and fight.

Carl's hard-held breath whistled out in a great sigh of relief. He had not been too afraid of the City men—perhaps they could have slain all his band, perhaps not—but the thought of killing men who fought for their own homes had been painful. Praise all gods, the witches had been bluffed!

He led the way to the well-remembered prison. The dwellers streamed away on either side, yelling and chattering. By the time Carl reached the jail, there was no sign of them.

Ronwy was straining against the bars. He reached through to take Carl's hands, and tears ran down his faded cheeks. "Praise all powers," he choked. "You've come, my son, you've come. Oh, praises be!"

"You haven't been hurt, sir?" asked Carl anxiously.

"No, no. They treated me well enough—afraid of my magic, I suppose. What brings you here again, Carl? What has happened? Fugitives passing by said the Lann were at Dalestown, and my heart grew sick within me."

Carl told the story as Sam and Ezzef broke open the door. When Ronwy emerged, he was trembling and leaned heavily on Tom's arm. "Outlawed?" he moaned. "Outcast from all tribes? Oh, this is bad, this is cruel!"

"It doesn't matter," lied Carl wearily. He was shocked to see how Ronwy had aged in these few days. But then, the old man had seen all he had striven for in his long life apparently brought to ruin. New hope should mean new life for him. "Now, my teacher, we are free to do as we have dreamed."

"I wonder. I wonder." Ronwy stroked his beard with thin,

shaking fingers. "This is a great and terrible thing you have taken on yourself, and I am not one of the old scientists. I am only one who has read, and imagined too much—become half a ghost myself in this ghostly place. We can try, yes, try our best—but time is short if we are to save the Dales, and I know so little . . ."

"We'll do it!" Carl's defiance rang out with a hopefulness he did not feel. "But come, let us rest you first, sir."

They went to Ronwy's home, closed and dusty since his imprisonment. The old man found wine and food, and Owl, who claimed to be a master cook, prepared a meal. That was cheering and strengthening to all, and they re-entered the street with higher hearts.

A strange procession met them, loaded wagons rumbling down the streets, armed men walking, women and children wailing their fright and sorrow. "What is this?" cried Ronwy. "What are you doing?"

His rival chief stopped and looked at him with hatred. "Your madness will bring the wrath of the gods down on the City," he answered. "We are leaving while there is still time."

"Leaving—but where will you go?"

"We will go to the Lann at Dalestown. If the gods do not smite you first, the Lann will avenge us."

"There will be no harm done," protested Ronwy.

"You were warned the last time. Thunder and lightning spoke, devils howled in the vault, and still your pride has not bent." The other old witch-man shook his head. "Perhaps the gods will not strike you even now. Perhaps they are so angered they do not care what ruin you bring on the world. But the Lann will care. They will help us."

"Hah!" muttered Owl. "The Lann are more scared of this place than you are."

"I don't know," said Tom worriedly. "Lenard, at least, fears nothing, and he may be able to break taboo with some of his men."

"Well, we can't stop the witches from going," answered Carl. "They are desperate enough to fight us and overwhelm us, or at least cut a way through to safety, if we try. We'll just have to hope they don't succeed with the Lann."

He and his men stood by Ronwy's door and watched the dwellers go past. Many cursed the invaders as they went by, and Ronwy bowed his head in grief.

"What have I done?" he whispered. "These are my people. What have I done to them?"

"Nothing, sir," said Carl as reassuringly as he could. "It's only their own ignorance driving them to this. And they'll come to no harm. Even the Lann have no reason to injure them, especially when they come as allies."

"But they curse me! They—hate me!"

"I've made myself an outcast from my own kind," answered Carl with pain. "The way of the pioneer is lonely. But they'll all bless us if we succeed. And if we don't—why, then nothing matters, I suppose."

"Yes—yes. You're right." Ronwy stared after the caravan until it was lost to sight.

"Come on," said Ezzef impatiently. "Let's see that vault."

The little band made its way down hollow streets, past emptily gazing walls and ruined splendors. Tom shook his head. "It'll take hundreds of years to build all this again," he said.

"Yes," answered Carl, "but we can make a beginning."

They came to the time vault and stood for a long while looking at it. "And that's the home of magic," breathed Nicky. "It's all in there—in that little place?"

"It will grow if we let it out," said Carl. "Grow till it covers the world."

Ezzef peered about with a soldier's eye. "We'll have to live right next to this, boys," he told the men. "I daresay we can clean out one of those rooms across the street for shelter, and bring in supplies of food and water in case we're attacked."

"Do you expect the Lann to come, then?" asked Owl.

"I don't know," said Ezzef practically, "but I'm not going to take chances. While you would-be magicians are snooping about inside the vault, the rest of us have work to do. We'll pile up rubble between the walls for a barricade." He looked keenly at Ronwy. "Just what do you expect to be looking for, anyway? What kind of weapon?"

"I don't know," admitted the old man. "I don't know at all."

CHAPTER 17

Return of the Lann

NIGHT had fallen, and fires blazed in the northern camp. A week of rest, lying at ease before Dalestown, jeering at the gaunt watchers on its towers, with nothing to do but sleep and play games and live well off the rich surrounding country, had given the Lann warriors restless new strength. They frolicked more wildly each day in the valley, wrestling, racing horses, shooting at targets, ranging afar to come back with a load of plunder from some undefended farmhouse, and each night, silence and slumber came later. On this evening, their foragers had brought in an especially fat herd of cattle and three wagonloads of southern wine, and the camp made merry.

Lenard stalked through the bivouac toward his father's tent. A frown darkened his face, and he nodded curtly to those who hailed him. He was in battle dress: his own spiked helmet and well-tried sword, a steel cuirass taken from a Dalesman's body, a great spear in one hand. But his looted clothes were the finest: a flowing purple cloak with golden brooch, a red tunic of fur-trimmed linen, fringed buckskin breeches, silver-studded boots with ringing spurs, and a heavy gold necklace about his corded throat.

On either side, the fires burned high, and the smell of roast meat still hung richly in the air. Ruddy light glowed off the rising smoke and splashed the faces of men sprawled near by. Although the Lann had weapons at hand, they were relaxed, flushed with the great bumpers of wine that went around the circle, and their hard, hairy bodies dripped gold and furs and embroidered cloth. The hubbub of voices, talking, laughing, shouting, roaring out songs to the thump of drums and the twang of banjos, beat like a stormy surf against Lenard's ears. It must be a terrible jeering music for the people in Dalestown, he thought briefly.

Behind him trotted a strange little man. His hair was not worn long as in the Dales or braided as among the Lann, but cropped close, and instead of trousers he had a ragged kilt flapping about his skinny legs. His tunic was of good material, but sadly tattered and muddy, half hidden by the bushy gray beard that swept down his chest. He had been disarmed and shrank timidly from the stares and raucous laughter of the barbarians who saw him.

The tent of Raymon loomed ahead, a square blackness against the night. Two guardsmen leaned on their pikes in front of it, looking wistfully at the revel. The Lann ruler himself sat cross-legged in the entrance before a tiny fire, smoking his pipe and tracing idle patterns in the ground with a knife blade. He was not a tall man, but broad of shoulder and long of arm, with keen, scarred features and hooded black eyes; his dark hair and beard showed only the faintest streaks of gray. He wore a furry robe against the evening chill, but under it one could see a painted leather corselet.

"Greeting, Father," said Lenard.

The older man looked up and nodded. He had never shown much warmth toward anyone, even his family. "What do you want?" he asked. "I'm thinking."

Raymon's thinking usually meant bad luck for his enemies. Lenard grinned for an instant, then sobered and lowered himself to the ground. His follower remained shyly standing.

"What do you plan?" asked Lenard.

"I'm wondering how long the town can hold out," said Raymon. "They're a stiff-necked bunch in there. They may eat rats and leather before they give in. I'd like to have this war finished within a month, so that we can move our people down here and get them well settled before winter. But is it worth-while storming the fortress— or can we starve it out in time? I haven't decided yet."

Lenard leaned forward, staring intently at the face dim-lit by the red coals. "I have news which may help you decide," he said.

"Well, so? Speak up, then. And who is this with you?"

"If it please you, honored sir, I am called Gervish, and I speak for the City—" began the stranger.

"Be quiet," said Lenard. To his father: "Yesterday one of our foraging parties to the north found a whole caravan of these folk, headed toward Dalestown. They said they came in peace to see us. This Gervish rode ahead with one of our men to carry the word. He was brought to me just now, and I saw this was something you should know about."

"Ah, so." Raymon's slitted gaze pierced the nervously hovering little man. "You're from a city? What city? Where? And why do you come to us, whom all others run away from?"

"Almighty lord, it is *the* City, the City of the ancients—"

"Be quiet, or we'll never get the story told." In brief, hard words Lenard related to his father the events which had caused the witch-folk to flee their homes. When he was through, he sat waiting for a response, but Raymon merely blew a cloud of smoke, and it was long before he answered.

"Hm-m-m," he said at last. "So those crazy boys are trying it again, eh? What's that to us?"

"It can be plenty," snapped Lenard. "You know the story of what went on before—how Carl scared off our men the first time with that magic light, and how there was thunder in the vault the second time. We may not get a third chance—not if Carl returns with the powers of the Doom."

"The City's been tabooed," said Raymon.

Lenard snorted in scorn and anger. "Yes, because that chicken-hearted Kuthay was frightened out of what wits he had. Oh, I admit I was scared too for a while. But I'm alive. Carl is no more a witch than I, but he's still alive too—and what's more, he's not afraid to go back there, even against his own tribe's will. I tell you, there are things in that vault which can be used against us—or by us—in a way nobody can yet imagine. If we don't get them, the Dalesmen will. And then woe for the Lann!"

Raymon turned to one of his guardsmen. "Fetch Kuthay," he ordered. "Also Junti, our highest-ranking Doctor. Quick!"

"Yes, sir." The warrior loped off and was lost in shadows.

"I'll go alone if I must," cried Lenard. "But—"

"Be quiet," said Raymon. "I have to think about this."

He sat impassively smoking while Lenard fumed and Gervish

cowered. It seemed an age before the red robes of Kuthay and stout, bald Junti came out of the night.

"Sit down," said Raymon. He did not apologize for disturbing their revel or sleep, whichever it had been. Among the Lann, the Chief held supreme power over even the Doctors. "We've something to talk over."

Kuthay started at sight of Gervish's gnomish features. "It's a witch!" he cried shrilly.

"That shivering dwarf?" Raymon sneered. "Sit down, I say, and listen to me." He gave them a crisp account of the story.

"We've nothing to fear, sir," said Kuthay a little shakily, when the tale was done. "The devils will take care of those Dalesmen."

"I wish they'd take care of you!" snorted Lenard. "You and your mumbo-jumbo magic and old wives' superstitions. This business may cost us the war unless we strike fast."

"What would you have us do?" asked Junti softly.

"Lift the taboo and then I'll take some men to the City and clean out the enemy there for good. After that it's ours!"

"The City—" wavered Gervish. "Sir, the City is our home—"

"The Lann will do what they please with your precious City. And with you too."

"I dare not," said Kuthay. His teeth were chattering. "I dare not let you go to that lair of devils. And bring them back here? All the gods forbid!"

"You'll let him if I say so," snapped Raymon. His voice grew shrewd. "But while we can change the law easily enough, can we change our men? Your followers from the last time have spread enough horrible stories about the City. Have we any warriors that would go there now?"

"I think many would," said Lenard thoughtfully. "First we should hold a great magical ceremony to arm us against all spells. Then we can take a large troop; there's confidence in numbers. And if we dangle all the wealth of the City before their noses, they'll follow me gladly enough. It must be stuffed with riches."

"No," wailed Gervish. He threw himself prostrate. "No, great sirs! We never meant that! The City is our home, and we are poor people with no other place to go."

"Be still or I'll have you run through!" snarled Raymon. Gervish's howls died to a tearful whimper.

"Hm-m-m." Junti stroked his chin. "I'm not too frightened of having people go there. As you said, Lenard, it doesn't seem to have hurt these Dale boys. But bringing things back—that's another matter. There's nothing understood about all this. You might be taking back the old plagues, or the glowing death, or—anything! No, no, I can't agree to your using the powers of the vault yourself.''

"But it's a threat otherwise," protested Lenard. "There'll always be a chance of someone like Carl going there and prowling about and turning the magic against us."

"Not if you destroy the vault."

"What? How?"

"Simple. Burn the books. Smash the machines. Fill the place with earth and stones." Junti nodded. "It'd be a worthy deed too. You'd be scotching the last seed of the Doom."

"Well—" Lenard hesitated. "I hadn't wanted to. I'd thought—"

"Enough," said Raymon. "It's a good plan. We're well enough off without risking new and unknown ways. Let it be thus, then. Tomorrow you Doctors hold a great devil-laying and spell-turning rite, and we'll call for about a thousand bold volunteers to ride with you to the City, Lenard. That should be enough to handle a score of Dalesmen! After you've taken care of them and wrecked that vault thoroughly, your boys can sack the place to their heart's content. Drag back whatever you find that can be used for siege-engines and the like—I understand the witches used to manufacture such for the tribes. If it's enough, we'll storm the town and burn it around the Dalesmen's ears and finish this war.''

Kuthay shuddered but was silent. Gervish, weeping, opened his mouth to protest again, saw the spearhead against his ribs, and closed trembling lips. Lenard scowled briefly, then his face cleared and he laughed, a hard, short bark of triumph.

In the morning, folk in the beleaguered town were wakened by the roll of drums and crash gongs. Men snatched weapons, cursing, deathly afraid that the long-awaited Lann assault was on them, and sped to their assigned posts. But Ralph, mounting one of the towers to peer over the valley, saw that it was not a summons to battle.

"What's going on, sir?" asked the guard beside him. "What are they doing out there?"

"I don't know." The Dale Chief had grown curt and grim since his son's flight. His eyes were haggard with sleeplessness as he stared at his foes.

The whole great army was massed about Raymon's tent, chanting and striking swords against shields in a clangor that drowned voices. A giant bonfire had been kindled and the red-robed Lann Doctors danced and drummed around it. As Ralph watched, he saw horses and cattle led up to the fire and saw a figure—he thought it was Raymon, but couldn't be sure—slash the throat of each sacrifice. Blood gushed into a bowl, from which the leader sprinkled it hot and red on the pressing warriors. Meat was hacked from the carcasses and thrown on the blaze, whose smoke mounted black and greasy toward heaven.

"It's some kind of rite," decided the Dale Chief. "They're preparing to do something. Storm us? No, I think not. The Lann never needed special ceremonies for a battle. I wonder—"

Afterward, Lenard harangued them from horseback. Slowly, a shout rose, swords waved in the air, spears were shaken fiercely and men roared. Some, Ralph saw, were edging away, silent, not liking whatever was being urged. But most howled approval.

It was near noon before the ceremony was finished. Ralph pondered the wisdom of a quick sally against that disordered throng. But no—with a half-mile of open ground to cover, the Lann would have plenty of time to meet him. Best to see what was brewing.

Lenard forced his steed through the mob, pointing to man after man, and each that he singled out, hurried away to get horses and war gear. Before long, a host of cavalry was assembled—nearly a thousand men, Ralph guessed dizzily. And their swift, sure readiness meant that they were of the best Lann troops, the trained warriors who had turned the tide against him at the last clash.

The division shook lances in air and hailed Lenard with a shout as he rode to the front. The rumble of hoofs drifted back to Ralph as they wheeled about together and trotted northward.

North!

"Where are they going?" wondered the guardsman. "What's their plan?"

Ralph turned away. His shoulders were suddenly bent, and horror was in his eyes.

"Carl," he groaned. "Carl."

• • •

The vault was dim, even with a dozen candles flickering about the littered workbench. The dank air, full of a harsh smell, made Carl's head ache. He looked past the great mixing kettle to Ronwy, who was scooping up the last grains of powder and stuffing them into a crudely fashioned metal canister.

"That's the last," said the old man. "There is no more sulfur."

Carl nodded wearily. "Perhaps a dozen bombs," he said. "No—fifteen, to be exact. I should know! Is that all we can do?"

"It's all the gunpowder we can make," shrugged Ronwy. He put a fuse in the canister, forcing it through a hole in the lid he had placed on the top, and tamped down clay to hold it. Carl took a pair of tongs and squeezed the container until it bent slightly, holding the lid in place.

It was fortunate, he thought, that the witch-folk had known sulfur. They bought it from traders and used it to smoke rats and mice from their storerooms. The bluff which had frightened away the Lann had used all the real gunpowder left in the vault, but an old book had described a way of making it. Saltpeter was another ingredient that had been in a small barrel here in the vault, and charcoal, which the Dalesmen themselves had prepared, was the third. The powders were weighed out on a scale, mixed wet, dried, and put into containers hammered from sheet metal dug out of the ruins.

Fifteen bombs—crude and weak, not even tested—all that the past six days of work had yielded. But there had been so desperately much to do: the formula had to be located in a stack of books Ronwy had once read but not remembered very well, a painful groping through many pages where half the words meant nothing; the powder had to be made, the metal found and beaten into shape. Carl's high-flying dreams had faded as he realized how hearbreakingly slow and difficult it would be to recreate the vanished past.

"Maybe that will be for the best," Ronwy had remarked. "We can't gain everything back overnight. We aren't ready for it. We should go slowly, take many generations on the task, so that we can learn the proper use of each new power before getting the next."

But—fifteen bombs!

"And now what can we do?" asked Carl. "It would take rare luck for this little bit of weaponry to decide a battle."

"I don't know." Ronwy sighed. "Make a balloon, perhaps. We would need a great deal of oiled cloth or fine leather, carefully

sewed into a bag, and a large basket to hang from it, and some
means of filling the sack with hot air—''

"We can't take a year for this!" cried Carl. Tears stung his eyes.
"The Lann aren't going to wait that long."

"No. No. But—''

"Carl—Carl—'' Tom came rushing down the stairs, wild and
white. "Carl, the patrol horn just blew! Someone's approaching!"

Carl rushed up into the noonday light and blinked at the hot
brilliance outside. His ears caught the warning blast now, from a
man perched as lookout high in one of the skyscrapers. Plunging
across the street, he burst into the room which his followers used for
living quarters. The men were already pulling on their armor, and
Carl dove for his.

"What is it?" barked Ezzef. "Who's coming?"

"I don't know," said the boy grimly, "but I'll bet it's an
enemy."

As he came out again, he looked to the defenses of the vault. His
men had wrought well. The open space between the two walls was
cleared of rubbish, which had been piled high to the rear to form an
almost unbreakable third wall; a jumbled wilderness of ruin beyond, where the Dalesmen had thoughtfully strewn broken glass
and sharp-edged metal, made it impossible to approach from that
side. On the front, where the old walls faced onto the street, a six-
foot barricade had been erected, stone and brick and timbers laid
solidly together, with only a narrow passageway between in to the
vault.

Nicky, who had been the lookout, came running as the last of his
comrades entered the little courtyard between vault and barricade.
"It's the Lann!" he panted. "A whole army of horsemen—hundreds of them—riding into the City!"

Carl grabbed his shoulders and shook him. "You're wrong!" he
shouted. "It can't be!"

"I tell you, I saw them," gasped Nicky. "And—hear?"

They heard it then, the rising and nearing thunder of trotting
hoofs, the banging of metal and the harsh clamor of voices. Man
looked at man, and friend shook hands with friend. For they were
twenty and the Lann were a thousand, and they did not expect to see
another sunrise.

CHAPTER 18

Battle of the Vault

A LINE of horsemen rode into view, their painted corselets agleam, their faces fierce under the helmets, lances aloft and hoofs ringing. Behind them were others, and yet others, stretching out of sight, and the noise of them was a rolling thunder.

Lenard rode in the van, haughtily erect on a great roan stallion, heavy saber in his right hand. It flashed up as he drew rein, and his cry went back over the pressing ranks: "Company halt!"

As one, the Lann stopped, horses stamping and snorting. Lenard sheathed his saber and lifted one hand. "Will you parley in there?" he called.

"If you wish." Carl stepped forth, standing between the thick walls of the barricade. "What do you want?"

"The vault and the City, of course." The Lann prince's hard face grew earnest. "Give up now, without a fight, and all your lives will be spared."

"Beware!" said Carl. His throat was dry, but he tried to be solemn and confident of manner. "The devils of the Doom are here."

Lenard threw back his head and laughed. "You won't frighten us that way, my friend," he cried. "Those who believe in such things have been given charms against all magic—and as for me, I've no more faith in those devils than you. Now, quickly, come out with your hands up, all of you. If you make any trouble, there'll be no mercy.''

"You can't use this vault," said Carl wildly. "You'll never understand—''

"I don't intend to use it. We're here to destroy the thing.''

"Destroy! No!" A thin shriek of agony ripped from Ronwy's heart.

"Yes! Now don't hold us up any longer. Come out from those stupid walls and let's be done with this foolishness.''

Carl shook his head, slowly and stubbornly. "I'm staying," he said.

"And I—and I—we'll all stay with you—'' The rumble of voices went from man to man of his followers.

"You're mad!" exclaimed Lenard. "It's death, I tell you—and all for nothing.''

"While we live, we'll fight you.''

"Very well, then!" His face contorted with rage, Lenard wheeled back to his men.

Carl drew a long shuddering breath. A tree growing in his little courtyard threw a dappled pattern of moving shadow on the sunlit walls. Tall clouds walked through a high, bright heaven. Oh, it was a fair world, a good life! But he couldn't give up. Not while the faintest gasp of hope remained could he surrender.

Three men could barely stand abreast in the entrance to the barricade. Carl, Tom, and Owl placed themselves there, shield locked with shield and swords out. Behind them were Ezzef, Nicky, and Sam, with pikes thrusting between the boys in the front rank. The other twelve disposed themselves about the courtyard, ready with weapons to repel any attempt at climbing the walls elsewhere; four, with bows, sprang to the flat roof of the time vault to shoot at the foe. Old Ronwy stood for an instant, bowed as if with over-whelming grief, then hurried into the vault and came back with an armload of bombs.

The Lann were handicapped by their very numbers, thought Carl, his last indecision and sorrow drowned in the high, taut thrum of battle. They couldn't mass horsemen in the street for one of their thundering attacks, nor could even one man gather full speed as he plunged across the width of the avenue against the defenders. But even so—even so—

Lenard and another rider trotted into sight, both carrying lances.

They went to the opposite wall, turned about, laid their shafts low, and spurred their animals with a sudden, shivering yell. Hoofs rattled as the charge came. Carl braced himself, waiting for the shock.

As the nearest lance head gleamed toward the Dale shields, the three pikemen lowered their twenty-foot weapons and planted the butts firm. The horses could have spitted themsleves on that bristling wall. Lenard cursed, reining in, his horse rearing. He poised his lance and threw it the short distance. It struck the wooden frame of Carl's shield with a dull blow, hung clumsily, and dropped out. Lenard drew his saber and hacked at the slanting pikeshafts. As he chopped at one and his companion at another, the third rammed suddenly forth. The other Lann warrior howled, his thigh pierced—his horse skittered away and a second rider leaped to take his place.

Lenard thrust suddenly between the pikeshafts. His horse loomed immensely over the defenders, and he struck downward with his saber. Carl met the blow with his own lifted blade, a wild roar of iron, sparks showering and the metal rebounding with shock. Grimly, Carl hewed, not at the man but at the horse. The animal screamed and stumbled. Lenard howled and smote again, his blow clanging off Tom's helmet. Ezzef drew his pike back a little and then brought the head murderously against the other foeman, pressing behind his Chief's plunging horse. It sank into the hairy throat and the man toppled from his seat. "First blood!" cried Ezzef.

Lenard's horse fell moaning to its knees. The Lann prince sprang from the saddle and hewed at Carl. Sword banged on sword. A fresh horseman was trying awkwardly to push his way in and fight. Lenard broke off the engagement, withdrew into the street, and bellowed at his man to come back with him. An arrow hummed past him, another one felled the retreating cavalryman, and Lenard turned and ran from sight.

"We drove them off!" panted Owl. His eyes blazed. "We beat them!"

"They'll be back," grunted Nicky. "They should've known better than to try horses against a defense like this, though."

Carl stooped over Lenard's wounded mount and looked into the tortured eyes. "I'm sorry," he whispered. "I'm sorry, old fellow." His knife gleamed, and the threshing animal lay still. Its body would form an extra obstacle.

"It'll be a foot assault next time," said Ezzef. He laid hi
unwieldy pike down and selected a spear instead. Nicky did like
wise, but Sam chose a long-shafted halberd.

The noise of the Lann drifted to them, angry voices and clashin
metal, but Carl could not hear what orders Lenard was giving
They'd be easy to deduce, though, he thought bleakly—attack
attack, attack, until sheer numbers overwhelmed a weary defense.

But there might be a chance. "Ronwy, are you there?"

"Yes." The old man was kindling a stick of punk. "I'm ready."

The Lann came into view. They were on foot now, with shield
and cutting steel in their hands, and it was such a swarming, boilin
mass of men that Carl could only see it as a confused storm. Th
clamor of voices rose to a terrible, high barking, yelping, the shri
war whoops of the Lann.

Arrows began to fly from the time vault, a gray sleet that struc
through steel and leather and flesh to send men reeling and dying
With a howl, the Lann charged.

Here they come!

Three of them abreast rushed in against the defenders in th
passageway. Ezzef's spear thrust out, catching one in the throa
Nicky's stab was turned by the shield of another man, but Sam
halberd reached out to bell on his helmet and hammer down hi
defense. The third struck against Carl, shield to shield, sword alof
and screaming down.

Carl took the blow on his armored left shoulder. He cut low
seeking the enemy's legs under the shield. The Lann roared. To
thrust from the side and brought him down. Another came leapin
over his body, and another and another.

A big man wielding an ax plunged against Carl. The boy
weapon sang, catching the wooden handle in mid-air, biting dee
into it. The warrior snarled, wrenched his weapon free and whirle
it aloft again. It crashed against Carl's shield. The frame on that sid
buckled, but the ax haft broke across. Carl's blade struck snakelik
against the man's arm. He fell, screaming, and Carl stooped to gra
his better shield. A barbarian roared, trampling over his dyin
comrade with a huge two-handed sword raised. Carl thrust upwar
with the point of his own weapon, catching the man in the armpi
The warrior staggered back, hindering those behind, and Carl g
the Lann shield free and onto his own left arm. Turning, he struc
from the side at the man engaging Owl and laid him low.

Another and another, a tide of faces and hammering blades. Carl hewed wildly as the enemy rose before him, not feeling the blows that rang and crashed off his own defenses, not feeling the cuts in his arms and legs. A northerner reached with a spear over the shoulder of one whom Carl fought, probing for the boy's head. The Chief's son struck at that shaft, beating it down, while he rammed his shield forward to hold back the swordsman. He hammered the spearhead down to earth, thrust out his foot, and snapped the shaft across. Sam's halberd clanged, dropping the barbarian swordsman. Carl chopped at the spearman before he could draw blade, sending him lurching back. A dying northerner stabbed upward with a knife. Carl saw the movement from the corner of an eye and stamped the man's hand down.

Looking backward, Carl saw that the enemy was trying to enter elsewhere. The cruelly jagged barricade could not be scaled, but the Lann were boosting each other over the ancient brick walls. The defenders in the courtyard fought desperately, hewing and thrusting and shooting as each new body loomed into sight and dropped to earth. Knots of battle raged back and forth, and the vault was splashed red.

"Ronwy!" gasped Carl. "Ronwy!"

A bright metal shape arched over his head, to fall among the enemy milling in the passage. A moment later came the shattering crash of explosion. Two more hurled bombs blew up. A ragged howl lifted from the Lann. They drew away, panting and glaring. Ronwy tossed another canister. It fell before the first men in that disordered crowd, and these suddenly turned and tried to break through those behind and escape. A flash, a boom, a swirl of smoke and brimstone—the Lann eddied in confusion, wild-eyed.

"Give me one of those!" exclaimed Ezzef. He took a bomb from Ronwy and threw it high above the wall, out of sight. A moment later came the scream of frightened horses as it went off among them. Men shouted, fighting their suddenly plunging mounts.

Carl drew a shivering breath. By all high gods, it had worked!

The dead and wounded lay thick before him. The battle in the courtyard died away as the last attackers were cut down. But four of the Dalesmen had fallen, and two others were out of action with wounds.

Tom stumbled suddenly, clutching at Owl for support. His face was white, and blood streamed from a slash in his leg. "Get him inside!" choked Carl. "Ronwy! Bandage that cut—"

"I will—I will." The old man eased Tom to the ground and ripped a piece off his cloak for a tourniquet.

"I can fight," whispered Tom. "I can still fight."

"Later," said Owl, inspecting the injury. "It'll heal up all right. But you're out of this fracas, my friend." He went back to his place, and Nicky took Tom's position.

Lenard raged among his men, yelling at them, ordering them forward again. The bombs had done little if any actual harm, Carl realized. It was the noise which frightened warriors and horses. And the Lann weren't so easily scared.

"I'll go myself!" Lenard ran toward the barricade. Two others followed, and then the rest shouted up their own courage and streamed in their wake.

Carl spread his legs widely, braced for the next shock. It came in a blurring roar of steel, whistling and crashing against his own hard-held defense, a weaving, flickering net of snakelike metal, and Lenard's taut grin bobbing behind a lifted shield. Carl struck back, hewing and stabbing and parrying. The Lann yelled and pressed forward. Sam groaned and sank slowly to earth, a spear wound in his side.

Crash! Crash! Crash!

The men attacking stopped in their onward surge. Someone wailed aloud. Lenard, raging, sprang against Carl anew, slipped in a pool of blood, and fell at the boy's feet. Lithe as a cat, he rolled free, leaped up, and was trapped in the backward rush of his men.

Crash! Crash!

A horse ran wild, pawing at the close-packed warriors and trampling them to the ground before it was killed. Carl wiped the sweat from his face and gulped air into raw lungs.

"One of them didn't go off," said Ronwy. His voice trembled. "We have four left."

Through the muttering army, Lenard strode, beating men with angry fists, urging them back again. Carl saw with wonder that they were close to blind panic. A fire leaped in him. It might work! Twenty men might drive off a thousand today!

"Forward, forward!" Lenard ran in the front. Slowly, a number of his warriors followed.

Ronwy hurled a bomb at them. As it clattered to earth, Lenard picked it up and tossed it back. It fell on the heaped bodies of the fallen and burst, metal fragments wailing and ricocheting. The Dalesmen stood firm, but the Lann flinched.

"Once more!" raged Lenard. "It didn't hurt you, did it? Once more and we'll have them!"

He plunged forward, saber gleaming. The Lann came after, a walking forest of swords and axes and spears. Carl staggered a little with weariness, thinking that this might indeed be the last assault.

The Lann prince charged him afresh. After Lenard came his men, swinging their weapons, but fear had blunted the attack and few tried to scale the walls to left and right. Carl's sword hummed, bouncing off Lenard's helmet. He felt the return blow bite deeply into his shield. Savagely, he cut low, and Lenard intercepted the sweep with his own blade just in time to save his legs. Swords locked together. They strained, grunting, glaring, and Lenard's greater strength slowly forced Carl's arm back.

Crash! Crash!

The barbarians howled, a single shuddering wail of stark terror, and fell away. Nicky and Owl laughed, closing in on the suddenly deserted Lenard. The northern prince cursed and retreated.

Crash!

The last bomb exploded amidst the enemy, scattering its terrible jagged fragments, and the host became a mob, screaming, fighting itself, clawing and trampling as it fled.

Carl gasped for breath. His head reeled and rang, and he began to tremble uncontrollably. He sat down where he was and stared into the courtyard.

His men had suffered cruelly. Not one but bled from a dozen wounds, and five lay dead and six could not stand. The arrows were exhausted, the swords nicked and blunted, the armor bashed and the shields splintered. But the fallen Lann were thick, and the Dalesmen managed a weary cheer.

"If they come at us again," said Ezzef grimly, "we're done for. This time they can't help carrying the day."

"We'll just have to hope they don't," answered Carl dully.

He sat listening to the howl of the mob. It seemed very far away. He must have dozed off, for he woke with a start as Owl touched his arm.

"Lenard's coming," said the farmer's son.

Carl got to his feet. The Lann prince was a gory and terrible sight where he stood in the avenue. His face was turned to his men, who were out of sight behind the looming walls but who had quieted down, and his voice lifted angrily.

"All right, I'll prove it! He's no more a witch than we are. I'll show you his magic won't help him. Then maybe you'll have heart enough to kill the rest of those pig-headed southlanders."

He turned to Carl and flashed a wolf's grin. "Truce!" he called. "I want a truce of battle while you and I fight it out alone!"

The boy stood stock-still. It was the custom among many tribes, he knew—single combat among the leaders before the real battle was resumed. He could not refuse this fight. Quite apart from custom, it would prove that he had no real magical powers to give him confidence; the Lann would take heart again and overrun the little defending force. But if he, Carl, failed in the duel, that too would inspire the Lann to a fresh and final attack.

"I'll go for you," whispered Ezzef.

"No, you can't," answered Carl. "I'm the one who's been challenged. Also, I'm the one they think is the witch—Ronwy and I, and Ronwy surely can't go. If I failed to meet this, it'd be the end for all of us."

"Come out, Carl, come out!" jeered Lenard. "Or are you afraid?"

"I'm coming," said the boy. He cast his battered shield to earth and took a better one from Ezzef. His sword was dulled with use, but so was everyone else's; it might still be sharp enough.

He felt no dread, he was past that now. But the weight of destiny was heavy on him as he walked out into the street.

CHAPTER 19

The Last Battle

THE sun was sliding down the last quarter of its journey toward darkness, and the mellowed, ivy-covered walls glowed with a golden light. Trees rustled here and there in the faint breeze. Through the hot reek of blood and sweat, Carl smelled a cool, damp breath of green earth and summer blowing from the great forest. He flexed his aching muscles, taking glory in their very throb and weariness. His heart beat steadily and strongly, air filled his breast and tingled in his veins. Every ridge on the sword haft under his fingers sent a message to him, telling of a real world, one to be grasped in the hands and known by the living body—a world of life and mystery, a world of splendor and striving and wistful beauty. Yes, it was good to live, and even if he was now to join the sun in an endless night, he was glad of what he had been given.

Lenard smiled at him and lifted his blade in salute. There was a strange warmth in his greeting: "I could almost wish you luck, Carl. You've been a gallant foe, and I would we had been friends."

The Lann stood waiting on either side of the cleared space, row on row of tensed and breathless men, still shaken by the thunder of the bombs. The defenders went outside their own barricade to watch.

"Go get him, Carl!" shouted Owl.

Carl crossed blades with Lenard. "Are you ready?" he asked.

"Yes," said the northerner. "Let's go!"

His saber slithered free and lifted for a downward sweep. Carl struck first, holding his shield up as he battered against Lenard's. The prince's blade rasped across that shield and slewed about toward Carl's thigh. The boy smote downward, beating the enemy weapon aside, and skipped back. Lenard rushed at him, blade howling. It crashed mightily against Carl's shield. The boy planted himself firm, and his lighter, straight weapon clashed against the saber.

Then they were at it, ducking and dodging, weaving around, and steel banging on steel. Carl's flickering blade sprang past Lenard's guard to slash the man's cheek. Lenard's saber answered, ringing on the Dalesman's helmet, bouncing from his shield. It struck the rim of that bullhide defense with a fury that dragged Carl's arm down. The Lann warrior grunted, thrusting forward, but his curved edge slid off the armored shoulder beyond. Carl hacked at the calf of his enemy's leg and felt his weapon bite through leather and flesh. The Dalesmen whooped.

Lenard growled and bored in, a sudden whirring, clamoring blur of attack. The blows hailed and thundered, shivering in Carl's muscles and bones. He tried to parry, and his sword was hammered aside. Lenard drove forward relentlessly. Carl stepped back, panting.

Whooo—bang! Carl's head reeled with the shock. Stars danced before his eyes. Lenard hewed at his ankles, drawing blood. Carl slashed at the barbarian's arm. The cut was deep, but the blunted edge would not bite well. Lenard grinned in fury and his snake's tongue saber blazed against the boy's defense. A ragged hole opened in the Dale shield, carved away by shrieking steel. Carl met the saber in mid-sweep, sparks and rattling. He ran backward as Lenard parried. The saber howled by his ear and raked down his sword arm.

He was fighting desperately now, against an older, heavier, more experienced warrior. The shock and thunder of blows was loud in his ears. He crossed blades and his own was hurled aside—almost wrenched from his hand. The frame of his shield gave away, a splinter stabbing his left arm. He threw the thing off, hurling it under Lenard's feet. The northerner tripped over it and crashed to the ground. Carl hacked at him, but the enemy shield turned his blow and Lenard scrambled up again.

"Well done!" he cried.

His saber whistled against Carl's now unshielded left. The boy retreated, weaving a barrier of flying metal to guard himself. The Lann army tightened and cheered, seeing him outclassed.

He couldn't go any farther. The wall of a building opposite the vault was suddenly against his back. Carl planted his legs firm and struck two-handed at Lenard, letting the northerner's blade smash at his own armored side. The straight sword whined against Lenard's incautiously exposed head. Blood ran free and Lenard's helmet rolled off. Carl had cut its chin strap but done little other harm. Lenard shook his head, bull-like, briefly dazed, and gave Carl a chance to slip back into the open.

Yelling, Lenard rushed him. Carl twisted his body sideways, holding his left arm out of danger. He thrust against the attacking barbarian, reaching for the eyes. Lenard nearly spitted himself, but he danced aside in time. Carl drilled in, pulling his dagger out with his left hand. Sword caught on sword, and Carl stabbed with the knife.

His thrust, awkwardly made, did little harm. Lenard broke free and crashed his shield-rim down on Carl's wrist. Numbed, the boy dropped the dagger. Lenard thrust close, sword spitting from behind his shield. Carl clinched again. Lenard thrust a sudden foot behind Carl's ankles and shoved. The boy went over on his back. Lenard sprang at him. Carl kicked with both feet. The kick thudded against Lenard's shield, driving him back. Carl rolled free and regained his stance, panting.

Lenard's blade sang against Carl's helmet. The Dalesman staggered, and the watching Lann cheered afresh. Carl lurched back, Lenard hammering his defense.

"Carl, Carl," groaned Owl.

Wildly, the boy held firm and battled. His breath was sobbing now. A wave of dizziness went through him and his knees shook. He was not afraid. There wasn't time for fear. But his body wouldn't obey; it was too tired.

He sent a mighty blow against Lenard's bare head. The shield came up to catch it, and the saber chopped for his neck. Carl ducked, letting the sweep ring on his helmet. He yanked his sword free and stabbed two-handed against Lenard's shield. The bullhide gave—but only a little, and Carl had to leap away before he was cut down.

His back was once more to the wall. He leaned against the old bricks and met the furious assault as it came. Steel whistled and belled, a flying blur.

Carl's sword met the thick edge of Lenard's saber, slid along it, and caught in a notch there. Lenard roared triumphantly and twisted with a skilled strength. The sword spun from Carl's sweat-slippery hand and went clanging to the street.

"Now you're done!" shouted Lenard. His saber lifted for the death stroke. The Lann howled their glee.

Carl sprang! He leaped against his enemy, one hand closing on the sword arm, one reaching for the throat. Lenard writhed, stepping back. Carl's right hand doubled into a fist and jolted a blow to Lenard's jaw. The northerner snarled and tried to jerk his weapon free. Carl tripped him, and they crashed to earth.

The boy clawed for the saber. Lenard's shield was pinned under the barbarian, holding his left arm useless. Carl's hands tugged at the saber haft. Lenard slipped his shield arm free and closed it about Carl's neck. The boy grunted, hammering a fist down on the fingers closed about the weapon. It suddenly clattered free as the two fighters rolled to one side.

Carl's fist smashed into the dark face that was now above him. Blood came. Lenard gouged for his eyes. Carl flung up an arm to protect himself, and Lenard twisted away, clutching after the saber. Carl got a scissor-lock about his waist and dragged him back.

The air was alive with the howling of the Lann. The Dalesmen strained forward, white and drawn of face. The combatants rolled in the street, fists and arms locked, battering, raging.

The flat of Lenard's hand struck Carl in the throat. Gasping with pain, the boy released his gripping arms. Lenard writhed half-free of the scissors-hold, reaching for the saber.

Carl surged up, clawing his way onto Lenard's back. He closed fingers in the barbarian's hair and smashed his enemy's forehead against the old pavement.

Lenard roared. Carl beat his head down again, and again, and again. Suddenly the warrior lay still.

"Carl, Carl, Carl!" whooped the Dalesmen.

The boy shook his head, now ringing and swimming with darkness. Thunder beat in his ears and blood dripped from his face to the street. Shuddering, he crawled free on hands and knees, looking up at the enemy host through ragged veils of darkness.

They surged uneasily, muttering, rolling wild eyes. Had the

boy's victory proved that he was a powerful witch, or did it mean nothing? But Lenard lay beaten, Lenard the bold who had egged them on in the teeth of angry gods. Their courage waned. There were so few Dalesmen to stand them off—but who knew what powers those few had ready to loosen?

Carl sat up, holding his aching head in both hands. The darkness was fading now, swirling from his eyes, but the thuttering and booming still went on. There were faint shouts and—

And they weren't within himself!

Carl staggered erect, not daring to believe. Above the Lann host, suddenly shrieking in alarm, there was the blowing of horns, the drumming of hoofs, the deep-voiced shouts of men. Far down the street, Carl saw a green and yellow banner advancing, floating against heaven. The noise of battle lifted as the newcomers fell on the Lann from the rear.

Dalesmen!

Carl reeled away from the sudden, trampling horde of spectators. Almost without thinking, he grasped Lenard by the hair and pulled the unconscous prince away from those frantic feet. Owl and Ezzef sprang out to help him back.

"Our people!" gibbered Owl. "Our people! I can't believe it!"

"Let me see—" New strength flowed back into Carl. Aided by his friends, he climbed up on the top of a wall from which he could see what was happening.

He recognized his father, mounted in the van of a Dale force that must have numbered some four hundred men. They were dusty, weary, their armor and bodies scarred with recent combat, their horses staggering in exhaustion, but they were hurling themselves against the enemy with a fierceness that rang between the ancient buildings.

The Lann at that end of the avenue had kept to their horses and were meeting the attack with the vigor of freshness. Behind them, their fellows rallied, pressing forward against this new menace and raising their own war shouts. Carl's new-found gladness turned to dismay.

The Dalesmen had come, yes—but they were tired, outnumbered two to one, moving against the most terrible foe of their history. Could they win? Would this prove only a trap?

CHAPTER 20

Twilight of the Gods

FROM his post on the wall, Carl saw Ralph plainly now. The Dale Chief was still mounted, a tall and terrible figure in travel-stained armor, hair flashing gold in the late sun. His standard-bearer rode beside him, but the rest of his army were leaping from their animals and thrusting ahead on foot.

A Lann cavalryman swung mightily at Ralph, sword whistling to clang against the Dalesman's blade. That steel seemed to come alive, howling and roaring, smashing down the northerner's guard and sending him to earth. A lancer thrust at Ralph. The Chief chopped out, hewing the shaft in two, and pressed against the man.

The Lann horseman edged back from the grimly advancing wall of pikes. In this narrow space, they had no chance against such an assault. Their comrades on foot yelled at them to get out of the way, and they too dismounted.

Now arrows began to fly over the heads of the front-rank Dalesmen, sleeting down among the Lann. A rattle of swords and axes lifted as the two lines met. The rearward Lann whooped, pushing forward, adding their own weight to the thrust against the Dalesmen. Their advance halted, the warriors of Ralph opened their ranks to let a line of their own swordsmen and axmen through the pikes.

Metal banged on metal and sheared in flesh. Ralph's horse neighed, rearing and trampling, while its rider's blade swung like a reaping scythe. The Lann attacked with steadily rising bravery, leaping over the bodies of the fallen, smashing against the Dale weapons, and slowly, step by step, they drove the newcomers back.

Ezzef groaned. "They're too many for us," he said. "Too many—it's all been for nothing, Carl."

"No—wait—what's this?" The boy peered down the street, shading his eyes against the western sun. "What are they doing?"

The double front rank of the Dalesmen stood firm, trading blow for blow, but their comrades behind them were withdrawing, racing down the street. Ralph himself pushed through his human wall to join those pulling back.

"Are they beaten already?" whispered Owl. "No, they can't be!"

Many yards of empty distance from the battle, the Dalesmen halted and wheeled about. Pikes reached through their massed lines, swords and axes swung free and bowmen and slingers loped in the rear. Ralph lifted his sword and plunged forward. His men poured after him, yelling.

The Dalesmen who had been standing off the foe suddenly sprang aside, crowding against the walls on either hand. Carl saw what his father's idea was, and he shouted with the men as that massed charge struck the Lann.

The four hundred men running together struck a terrible blow whose hammer-noise trembled in the earth and lifted up to heaven. Pikes were driven like battering-rams, smashing through all defenses to shatter the first barbarian lines. Those behind reeled from the shock, forcing their own rearward men farther back. A gray storm of arrows rained on the suddenly confused Lann army, and the hewers of the Dales thundered against them and hurled them into each other.

For long moments, the struggle went on; the Lann in retreat before the smashing, sundering Dalesmen, their ranks crumpled, panic running blindly among them. They had been shaken by powers of magic; they had been made leaderless; they had been assailed by an enemy they thought safely bottled up. It was too much!

With a single mob howl of utter dismay, the Lann turned and fled.

The Dalesmen pursued them, smiting without mercy, taking revenge for all the bitterness they had suffered. Battle snarled past the time vault, turning to butchery, and went on down the street and lost itself in the forest as the Lann scattered.

Carl sprang from the wall into Ralph's path. "Father!" he cried. "Father, you came!"

"Oh, Carl, my son, my son—" The Chief dismounted and embraced him in trembling arms.

Night came, with stars and moon and a singing darkness. Men pitched camp in the ruins and slept for utter exhaustion. To the wounded, Lann and Dale alike, the gentle night gave rest and forgetfulness; over the dead it drew a shroud. The moon swam high in a winking sea of stars, touching leaves and old walls with a ghostly silver.

Peace—

Some were still awake, sitting about the hearth in Ronwy's home. A fire crackled before them, the light of candles touched their faces and shone in their eyes. Ralph was there, sprawled in a seat of honor with his sword across his knees. Carl sat by him, holding one of Ronwy's books in his lap and stroking its faded cover with shy fingers. Tom and Owl, the former insisting that his wounds were mere scratches, lay on the rug. Lenard, his head swathed in bandages, sat gloomily in a corner. The little witch-man, Gervish, who had followed Ralph to the City, hovered about trying to be of service to someone.

Ralph was telling the story of his arrival. "Even if you haven't won anything else, boys, you saved us by drawing off a thousand of the best Lann," he told them. "When I saw them go away, I was sure they were bound for the City. I waited till they were safely distant, then led all our men out against those who remained. And this time we won! We broke them in the field. When their Chief fell, they scattered before us. Now they're streaming homeward, beaten, harried by our forces just so they won't get ideas about turning back. We've won!"

"My father," said Lenard dully. "He's dead?"

"Yes," said Ralph.

"I—I'm sorry," whispered Carl.

"Oh—I'll see him again—in Sky-Home after I die." Lenard tried to smile. "That makes me Chief of the Lann, doesn't it? A prisoner Chief—" He bowed his head, then looked up with a sigh.

"But I may be better off this way. This defeat may well break up the confederation. . . ."

Ralph went on: "Well, our folk were naturally full of glee and ready to lick the world. I took advantage of that—made them a speech pointing out that a thousand warriors were still loose up in the City, perhaps brewing magic against us and in any case nothing we wanted running free in the Dales. I got enough lads to follow me so I thought we'd have a chance. We hurried, I can tell you! We killed horses and nearly killed ourselves, but it was worth it."

"The taboo?" breathed Carl.

"Donn came with us. I thought you knew that." Ralph looked keenly at his son. "Never thought the old fellow could match the pace we were setting, but he did. I left him talking to your friend Ronwy, and—" He looked at the door. "And here they are!"

The two old men entered, side by side. Donn paused in the doorway, looking beyond the chamber to a dream. An almost holy light shone in his eyes.

"I have been in the vault," he whispered. "I have seen the treasure there, looked at the high-piled wisdom of the books. I have read the words of that unknown who gave it to us, and I have talked with this wise one here—" He shook his head, and a smile hovered about his thin lips. "There is no evil in the vault. There is only evil in the hearts of men. Knowledge, all knowledge, is good."

"Then you'll lift the taboo?" cried Carl joyously.

"I shall urge the Council to do so, and I know they will. Afterward, Carl, you shall have whatever help the Doctors can give out of their little wisdom, to rebuild the old world as you have longed." Donn's smile became almost a grin. "Even if I myself wouldn't admit my error, which I freely do, four hundred lusty Dalesmen who've been to this place of wonder and come to no harm would have something to say about it!"

It was as if a great brooding presence were suddenly gone, as if the wandering night breeze sobbed in a new loneliness. The gods were doomed—the cruel, old pagan gods of human fear and human ignorance felt their twilight upon them. And the darkness which dwells in every mortal heart cried out to the dying gods.

Gervish was kneeling at Ronwy's feet. "Forgive us," he murmured brokenly. "We were wrong, all of us were wrong. The Lann from whom we sought aid would have ruined us. The Dalesmen, your friends, saved us; and the magic is not evil. Be our Chief again!''

Ronwy lifted him. "Let there be no talk of forgiveness," he smiled. "We've too much to do even to remember the past, let alone judge it. But bear this in mind, Gervish, and tell it to the pepole: We of the City will be among the first to benefit from the released powers. Above all, the lifting of the taboo makes us a tribe like any other, who can walk like men instead of shunned and hated outcasts."

Lenard spoke with sadness. "It seems that everyone but my poor Lann will gain from this." A dark flash of menace: "They'll come back someday!"

Ralph shook his head. "I don't know what to do about you people," he said. "It's true, I suppose, that you were driven by great need to attack us. But the same force will drive you against the south once more, and once again after that. If we are not to be plagued by endless wars—what can we do?"

"The vault is the answer!" cried Carl eagerly. "Look, Lenard, there are plans and models in it designed for the use of people like ourselves, people who can't hope to master the greatest of the ancient powers for many years yet. There are things we can do and build right now!"

"Such as what?" challenged Lenard. Despite himself, there was a quickening in his own voice.

"Oh, many things. For example, there's something called a schooner, which can sail against the wind—yes, I know it sounds fantastic, but I'm willing to try! They'll at least sail rings around the clumsy luggers the coastal tribes use today. Make them big enough, and you Lann can open trade, fisheries—why, even new lands to colonize! Then there are ways to use wind power for grinding grain, when you don't happen to have water power handy; and the rules by which you can breed better plants and animals; and means to prevent some of the diseases that now scourge us all. Oh, it's a long list, and I'll bet we find a lot more in that vault when we get it really well explored.

"Give us a chance, Lenard." Carl's tones beat urgently against the barbarian, who sat with lowered head. "You're Chief up there, now that your father's gone; they'll listen to you. Swear a truce with us. Swear it now and then go back and make your people keep it!"

"We may be able to hold out for three years—" said Lenard doubtfully.

"That's fine," said Carl. "Oh, that'll do! We'll have *something* to show you by that time, something to share with you, that you can use to better your own lot without taking from anyone else."

"I'll arrange for food to be sent to you during the truce," said Ralph. "You can pay us back later, when these old things make you better able to afford it. Peace," he added, "is kept by the good will and strength of the peaceful."

"I'll do it!" exclaimed Lenard. He thrust his hand out. "By Jenzik, you've been brave enemies and I think you'll be good friends!"

Carl and Ralph clasped hands with him. Gladness filled the boy's heart.

It would be a mighty task, this rebuilding. Lifetimes must pass before it was completed. But what better work could anyone ask for?

Carl went softly to the door and opened it and looked out into the summer night. It was dark now, but dawn was not far off.

SCIENCE FICTION BESTSELLERS
FROM BERKLEY

Frank Herbert

DUNE   (03698-7—$2.25)

DUNE MESSIAH   (03930-7—$1.95)

CHILDREN OF DUNE   (04075-5—$2.25)

Philip José Farmer

THE FABULOUS RIVERBOAT   (03793-2—$1.75)

TO YOUR SCATTERED BODIES GO   (03744-4—$1.75)

NIGHT OF LIGHT   (03933-1—$1.75)

Robert A. Heinlein

TIME ENOUGH FOR LOVE   (03471-2—$2.25)

STARSHIP TROOPERS   (03787-8—$1.75)

THE PAST THROUGH TOMORROW   (03785-1—$2.95)

Send for a list of all our books in print.

These books are available at your local bookstore, or send price indicated plus 30¢ for postage and handling. If more than four books are ordered, only $1.00 is necessary for postage. Allow three weeks for delivery. Send orders to:

Berkley Book Mailing Service
P.O. Box 690
Rockville Centre, New York 11570

REMEMBER IT DOESN'T GROW ON TREES

ENERGY CONSERVATION -
IT'S YOUR CHANCE TO SAVE, AMERICA

Department of Energy, Washington, D.C.

A PUBLIC SERVICE MESSAGE FROM BERKLEY PUBLISHING CO., INC.